Love Ma
House a F

Home to Collingsworth
Book 3

by

Kimberly Rae Jordan

THREE**STRAND**
P R E S S

A CORD OF THREE STRANDS IS NOT EASILY BROKEN.

A man, a woman & their God.
Three Strand Press publishes Christian Romance stories
that intertwine love, faith and family.
Always clean. Always heartwarming. Always uplifting.

❧ Chapter One ❧

JESSAMINE Collingsworth stepped into the bedroom and set down the boxes and the handful of garbage bags she carried. She wrinkled her nose at the stale air that filled the room. These rooms had been closed up since Gran's death. Jessa's last time in the large suite had been to pick out an outfit for Gran's burial. She would have been content to leave them for a while longer, but even from beyond the grave Gran was forcing the issue with her renovation plans.

The room still looked like it was all original to when the house had been built. Jessa wasn't aware that Gran had done any updating to her suite of rooms except for a new toilet and bathtub in the master bath. At one time it had probably been considered beautifully decorated, but now with its antique pieces of furniture and heavy curtains over the dark walls, it just looked dated.

A light layer of dust coated the top of Gran's dresser. It wasn't much, but it would have driven her crazy. Even after she'd retired from taking care of the rest of the house, Sylvia Miller had come to the manor once a week to clean Gran's rooms. She had been the only one Gran had trusted to care for her things, but Jessa was sure her grandmother had paid her well for her work.

With a sigh, Jessa looked around, trying to gauge just how much stuff there was to sort through. Gran actually had a suite of rooms which consisted of a decent sized bedroom, a smaller sitting room, a master bathroom, and a small room that had once been used as a nursery.

As she stood there, Jessa thought again about keeping this suite as it was. Not the décor, but the setup. Though she hadn't spoken to the others about it yet, she was considering turning the manor into a bread and breakfast. Having a suite of rooms like this for herself and, hopefully one day, her husband, would be ideal.

Violet would be moving out once she and Dean got married. Though there was no engagement yet, Jessa was sure it was just a matter of time. Rose was going to move in with Laurel and Matt, which just left her and Lily. And Cami. But she was pretty sure whatever plans her younger sister had, they didn't involve moving into the manor on anything but a temporary basis.

She would have to ask Lance for another look at the plans to see what Gran had done to her set of rooms. If she hadn't left them in the plans, Jessa hoped Lance would be willing to consider some changes to accommodate keeping them.

Lance. Even just the thought of him caused her stomach to knot. It looked like he had managed to get on with his life quite nicely after he'd dumped her. Back then she'd told people they had broken up because of Gran. The truth was he'd been the one to end it. Gran had made her dislike of him clear when she'd found out about them dating. And when she'd come upon them just as he was leaving after breaking up with her, she'd yelled at him to never come back. So most people believed her story that Gran had forced them to break up, but, unfortunately, she knew the truth.

Though she noticed he didn't wear a ring, she knew he'd gotten engaged shortly after that horrible night when he had broken things off. So while he may have been the love of her young life, she certainly hadn't been his. It had been bad enough that the relationship had ended, but the knowledge that she could be so easily replaced had hurt more than anything. He'd said it was because they were moving, but with the way things had unfolded after that, it was more likely that he just hadn't loved her. She had been dreaming of a future with him. It had no doubt been too much to expect of an eighteen year old boy.

"Jessa?" A knock accompanied her name. She turned to see Laurel standing in the doorway. For all that she'd gone through in the past few weeks, her sister looked so much better.

She smiled at her. "Hey. What's up?"

Laurel stepped inside and looked around. "This room used to scare me."

"Yeah. It's not the most welcoming place," Jessa agreed. "If only these walls could talk though."

Laurel visibly shuddered. "I'm not sure I'd want to hear what they'd have to say."

Jessa laughed. "True. I'm just trying to get my nerve up to start going through all of Gran's stuff."

"Do you need some help?" Laurel asked as she ventured to Jessa's side.

"It would definitely go faster," Jessa admitted.

"Oh, I almost forgot the reason I came up in the first place," Laurel said as she held up her cell phone. "Did you get Cami's text?"

"No. I heard an alert on my way here, but my hands were full, so I didn't check it." Jessa pulled her phone from her pocket. "What's up with our absent sister?"

"She said she's coming in on Thursday and wondered if someone could pick her up."

"Finally she makes contact, eh? Nothing like leaving it until almost the last minute," Jessa said, trying to stem the irritation she felt toward her younger sister.

"Yeah, I know, but at least she's coming. I thought I could drive down on Wednesday, spend the night and come back on Thursday with her."

Jessa nodded. "That would be good. I imagine you'd like to spend some time with Matt."

A smile brightened Laurel's face and her eyes sparkled. "Yes, I would. I wish he had let me go back with him today, but he was sure I wouldn't rest much there like I would here. However, I think he'd let me come home for one night."

"And you're in luck. Rose won't even bug to go with you this time," Jessa told her.

"Why's that? I thought I might have to bribe her."

"She has a birthday party and a sleepover on Wednesday. She's been looking forward to it since the end of school so she won't want to miss that."

Laurel nodded. "I remember her mentioning that the other day. I'm glad she'll have something to do while I'm gone."

Jessa frowned. "Are you up for the drive though?"

"I think I'll be okay. Every day I'm feeling stronger. But, if necessary, Cami can drive back."

"That's true." Jessa looked around the room again before walking to one of the windows and throwing open the curtain. She lifted the window to let some fresh air into the room. "Guess we'd better get started, if you're up to it."

"I am. Can't lift anything heavy, but I can certainly sort stuff."

"How about you work on the bathroom?" Jessa suggested. "I guess most stuff should be tossed, but anything new you find we can donate."

Jessa carried a one of the boxes into the bathroom and got Laurel set up to begin sorting in there. She returned to the bedroom and debated where to start. The few boxes she'd brought upstairs weren't going to even put a dent in what needed to be moved out. With a sigh, she walked to the large closet and began to take clothes off hangers and lay them on the big bed. Once the hangers were all empty, she folded the outfits carefully and put them in the black garbage bags. They would hold a lot more clothes than the boxes would. While Gran no doubt would have objected, putting the clothing in the garbage bags was the easiest way to pack them away.

As she folded the clothes, Jessa recognized so many of the outfits Gran had worn over the years. She ran her fingers over the soft fabric of a silk shirt. Gran had always cared very much about her appearance. Her hair and makeup had always been done perfectly if there was any chance she'd see anyone outside the family. And her clothes had been nothing but the best.

"It is expected of us as Collingsworths to look the part of a founding family," Gran had always said. Although who had decided what a founding family had to look like was still a mystery to Jessa. She just hoped there were others out there who liked to dress like Gran, because there were a ton of clothes to donate.

Abandoning the pile of clothes for a moment, Jessa walked to the bathroom to check on Laurel.

"Gran has more new products than you might have thought," Laurel said as she waved her hand at a counter full of bottles. "Did she have a bit of a shopping problem?"

Jessa shrugged. "Not that I'm aware of, but I wasn't always with her when she shopped."

"There's a lot to throw out, but also plenty to keep or donate. You might want to look through them before you decide. There's some nice stuff here."

"Feel free to keep what you want," Jessa told her. "And speaking of donating, would you be willing to take a load into a thrift store in the Twin Cities when you go?"

"Sure, but why not donate here?" Laurel asked as she checked another bottle before tossing it into the trash bag.

"I think Gran would come back to haunt me if I let her clothes go to a local thrift store. She'd probably be afraid that people would recognize them and buy them with evil intent."

Laurel laughed. "Like what? She's already passed on. Not much more anyone could do to her."

"True," Jessa said. "But I'd still feel more respectful of her memory if we didn't donate her more recognizable things to the store here. Stuff like the cosmetics and toiletries I don't have a problem with and even the furniture if we decide to get rid of some of it. But her more personal things...I think they should go somewhere else."

"You're probably right," Laurel agreed. "Sure. I can take whatever you've got ready to go by then. We can fill the car right up. They are usually pretty good about helping unload stuff at the one store I've donated to before."

"Thanks. I would feel a lot better doing it that way." Before returning to her own sorting, Jessa said, "Be sure to take a break if you need one. I don't want you to overdo it. Matt would be one very unhappy brother-in-law if I let that happen."

They worked in silence for another hour before Laurel came out of the bathroom. "I think that's pretty much all done. I'm going to go downstairs and start lunch. Want anything?"

"Sure. I'll be down in a few minutes. Just want to finish this up."

Alone in the room, Jessa pulled out her cell phone as she sank down on the edge of the bed. She debated making the call, but really did want to preserve what she could of the bedroom suite before it was too late.

Out of practicality—or so she'd told herself—Jessa had put Lance's cell number in her phone after he'd left them with a business card at their last meeting. Her thumb wavered over his name, but then she touched the screen and pressed the phone to her ear.

❧ Chapter Two ❧

*E*VANSTON," he barked when he answered.

"Lance?" Jessa asked since she didn't immediately recognize his voice.

"Yep. How can I help you?" His words were brusque with a tinge of impatience.

"Sorry to bother you. It's Jessa. Collingsworth." She tacked the last name on just in case he knew a whole bunch of other women named Jessa.

There was a beat of silence before he spoke again. This time his tone was less harsh and more approachable. "Jessa! This is a surprise. What can I do for you?"

"Am I interrupting? You can call me back at another time if that's more convenient."

"Nope. Now's good," he said. "What's up?"

"I've been working upstairs in Gran's room getting ready for the renovations, and I'm wondering what had been planned out for this area of the house in the designs you showed us."

"Well, we're going to be gutting it completely, but your grandmother still wanted to keep it as a separate suite of rooms. She asked me to design it to enlarge all the rooms, including the bathroom, and give it a better entrance."

"So you'll be making the bedroom, sitting room and bathroom bigger?"

"Yes. She also wanted a walk-in closet added."

"And what about the smaller room connected to the bedroom?" For reasons she didn't quite understand, she didn't want to call it by its name.

"The nursery?" Lance asked, naming it for her without hesitation.

"Yes. The nursery."

"Your grandmother also insisted that be left in place, but she wanted it opened up a bit more with a window. To let in more sunlight, she said."

"And what do you mean by a better entrance?"

"Well, I believe right now the main door opens into the bedroom, correct?"

"Yes. All the other rooms connect off the bedroom."

"She asked me to create an entrance that would allow access to the sitting room and nursery without having to go through the bedroom. They would still interconnect, but in the new plans, someone could go into either of those rooms without having to go through the bedroom first."

"Okay. Thank you."

"Does that fit with what you were wanting?"

"It's actually more than I had thought about. I just wanted to make sure that the suite stayed intact."

"Yes, it will stay intact, but the one bedroom next to it will be gone in order to make room for the enlarging of the master suite." He paused and then said, "Your grandmother mentioned something about you wanting to turn the manor into a bed and breakfast. I think setting up this suite was her way of helping with that."

His comment caught Jessa off guard. "Really? I had mentioned it to her in passing a couple of times, but always knew she'd never go for it as long as she was alive."

"Yes. I can imagine she wouldn't take too well to having strangers in her home."

"I figure it's a shame to waste so much space. It's full now, but I'm assuming Violet will be moving out at some point. Laurel and Matt will be taking Rose back to Minneapolis with them, and I sincerely doubt Cami will ever come back to Collingsworth to stay. So it will just be me and Lily, and this is too much house for only two people. I figure that with the college there are probably parents coming to town that might want to stay in a B&B instead of a hotel."

"I'm sure you're right, but why is Rose going to live with Laurel?" Lance asked.

"She is Rose's mother."

After a beat of silence, Lance said, "No kidding?"

"Nope. Gran didn't want people to think Laurel might be like Elizabeth, so she just told everyone our mom had dropped off yet another baby. Now with Gran gone, Laurel wanted Rose to know the truth."

"That's great." Lance said. "Hang on."

Jessa heard some muffled conversation and just before Lance returned to their conversation she heard him clearly say, "You'd better put it back with the rest of the toys before your mom gets home. She won't be happy at the mess you've made."

A hard knot formed in her stomach. He was with a child. Was it his?

"Well, it sounds like you're busy," Jessa said. "Thanks for the information about the suite. Cami is arriving on Thursday, so we're on schedule to start next week. We're working on getting Gran's rooms cleared out now."

"Okay, sounds good. I'll give you a call at the end of the week to firm up the details."

Jessa ended the call and sat staring at her phone. What had she expected? Still, after all these years, there was a part of her that found Lance fascinating and appealing. She'd never let anyone know how devastated she'd been when he'd ended things, but to this day she could feel the pain of that night as clearly as if it was happening right at that moment. How she was going to make it through the upcoming weeks with him around was beyond her.

Her phone chirped, and she looked down to see a text from Laurel. *Lunch is ready whenever you want to take a break.*

Definitely ready to leave the dark, depressing room and her thoughts, Jessa washed up and joined Laurel and Rose for lunch.

After lunch, though she knew she should return to Gran's rooms to keep working, Jessa went instead to her greenhouse. The afternoon was warm, but the trees that lined the paved path leading to the greenhouse gave protection from the sun. The walkway was wide enough for a truck to drive to and from the structure to pick up produce and flowers and drop off soil and fertilizer.

Though she loved working with nature, she wasn't as enamored with the actual outdoors the way Violet was. Jessa had no desire to climb mountains or shoot the rapids, but give her some rich soil and seeds, and she was in her glory.

Once inside the large structure, Jessa made her way along the center aisle to the back of the building. An earthy aroma filled the air, and she breathed deeply of it as she settled on a stool at the large wooden work bench. The contrast between this light-filled, green luscious space and the dark, gloomy bedroom of Gran's was marked. Everything in the greenhouse spoke of life while that room back at the manor only carried an air of death.

This greenhouse had been Gran's gift to her, although

Jessa had long thought it was more of a bribe to keep her close to home. It was an expensive project, and Jessa had been determined that if she was going to pursue this, she wanted to do it right. She'd researched it extensively for almost six months before approaching people in Minnesota who had knowledge of greenhouses used for year round growing in their zone three location.

When she'd given Gran her final plan for the greenhouse and what was necessary for heating, cooling and the water delivery system, Jessa had been sure she'd back down because of the cost. But if there was one thing the older woman appreciated, it was a well thought out, well organized plan, and Jessa had given her just that. Best of all, it had tied in well with the landscape design degree she'd been able to obtain through Collingsworth College.

It had taken several years to get the greenhouse functioning at the level it did now. Lots of experimentation had gone on, but the result was an operation that ran smoothly. She had people who came in and helped when necessary. And classes from the local schools would often come by to learn about the different aspects of growing their own food. If she weren't already well off, this venture certainly wouldn't have made her rich, but it was finally getting to a place where it generated enough money to pay those who came to help out.

As she looked over the notes left by the workers who had come earlier in the day to pick up produce for the shop, Jessa tried to block out all the other stuff that was going. *Gran's room. The renovations. Lance.* She didn't want to deal with any of it right then.

"Jessa?"

At the sound of her name, Jessa turned then slid off the stool. She walked to where she could see to the front of the building. She immediately recognized the tall lanky figure of Gareth Williams.

"Hello, Gareth," she called out as she moved toward him. "I didn't realize you were coming out today."

He smiled at her as she approached. "I ended up not having a class this afternoon, so thought I'd take advantage of your invitation. Your sister sent me out here. Is this a good time?"

Jessa nodded, enjoying the sound of his Australian accent. "Yep. Although you're not going to be able to see the greenhouse in full operating mode. Our outdoor gardens are in full swing now."

Sticking his hands in the pockets of his worn jeans, Gareth looked around. The last time she'd seen him he must have come straight from teaching because his attire now was a lot more casual than it had been then. His long wavy hair hung loose around his shoulders. The jeans he wore had holes in the knees, and he wore sandals.

"This is still a pretty impressive operation you have here." He moved to one of the sections that still had several rows planted. Jessa followed him, answering his questions and sharing her experiences in setting the greenhouse up.

Over the next hour, they did a tour of the structure, and Jessa found it exciting to share her knowledge with someone who clearly shared her passion for plants and growing things. Most people in Collingsworth had thought she was a little nuts when she'd started out, but now they enjoyed the fresh vegetables and fruits in the middle of winter. She also had some older people who just liked to come spend time in the greenhouse in the midst of their coldest season, claiming it did their soul good.

"You've impressed me, dear," Gareth said as he surveyed the greenhouse from her work area. His green gaze met hers. "I'd love to talk more. Dinner?"

"Tonight?"

"I realize it's short notice." He gave her a wink. "But finding you in this small college town is like finding a rare orchid in a common garden."

Jessa couldn't keep the smile from her face. "You have a way with words. Are you an English professor?"

"Yes. That is one of the subjects I teach," he said. "So? Dinner tonight?"

"I'd like that."

"You know this area better than me, so you pick where you'd like to go," Gareth said. He handed her a card. "Here's my cell number. Give me a call when you decide."

Jessa nodded. "I'll walk you out."

"There's no need. I've already taken a chunk of your time. I'll see you later."

Jessa walked as far as the entrance of the greenhouse and then watched him until he disappeared around the curve in the walkway. She tried to return to the work she'd been doing before Gareth had appeared, but finally gave up and returned to the house.

Violet and Laurel were talking in the kitchen, but abruptly stopped when they spotted her. The excitement she'd been feeling dropped a notch as she took in their expressions.

"What's wrong?" she asked.

"Nothing." Laurel gave her a smile that didn't quite back up her response.

Jessa looked at Violet, figuring of the two, she would be more forthcoming. "What's wrong?"

Violet sighed. "Well, neither of us really like that Gareth guy. He just gave off some weird vibes."

Jessa fought the urge to roll her eyes and tried to ignore the flutter of irritation at her sister's words. "I found him to be quite engaging. It's not often I find someone I can talk to about something I love."

"You mentioned he was into gardening too, right?" Laurel asked.

Jessa could tell Laurel felt bad about not being more positive regarding Gareth. "Yes, he is. And we're going to go out for dinner tonight to talk about it some more."

Violet's brows drew together at her statement. "Are you sure that's a good idea?"

"Seriously?" Jessa didn't bother to hide the irritation this time. "I'm just going out for dinner with the guy. It's not like he's proposed marriage or anything."

"We're just worried about you," Laurel said, laying her hand on Jessa's arm. "You've had a lot going on."

"Yes, I have, which is precisely why I need this evening out." Jessa scowled at Violet. "Besides, don't I at least deserve a shot at a relationship?"

"Sure you do," Violet said. "I'm just not sure about this guy."

"Well, then I guess it's a good thing you've already found your Prince Charming." Jessa knew she was coming off snarky, but it was hard to not get irritated at her two sisters who were happily in relationships trying to warn her off a guy who had done nothing to deserve their judgment.

Violet sighed. "Sorry, Jess. I hope you have a nice dinner with him. I'm glad you've met someone who can share something you're so passionate about. I know that's important."

"Where are you planning to go?" Laurel asked.

"I'm not sure," Jessa said. She knew her sisters were attempting to make up for their negative reaction, but the irritation she felt toward them lingered. Before she could say anything further, her cell phone rang. "Hello?"

"Hi, Jessa. It's Stan." He paused then said, "Everything okay?"

Realizing her irritation must have been evident in her greeting, Jessa let out a sigh. "Everything's fine. Just dealing with stuff."

"Well, I hate to add to your plate, but I've been in contact with Will and his family."

Jessa sank down on one of the stools at the counter. "Is

there a problem?”

“Not really. Will would like to come for the next month or so and work at the manor alongside you girls. He’s between a couple of jobs, so the timing is good. Would you be okay with that?”

“Let me talk to the others, and I’ll let you know. I don’t think it will be a problem though. Can I call you back in about half an hour?” After Stan agreed, Jessa hung up and explained the situation to Laurel and Violet. “So are you guys okay with him being here for the month?”

“If Gran’s ultimate plan was to bring us all together, I think it’s a good idea to include Will in this,” Violet said.

“Okay. I’ll let Stan know. I guess one of us will have to go get him,” Jessa pointed out.

“If he flies in on Wednesday or Thursday morning, I can pick him up,” Laurel said. “And I guess if he flies in later in the week, he could come up with Matt. He will be driving up on Friday.”

“I’ll give Stan those two options to see if they can work around those. If not, we’ll figure something else out.” Jessa placed the call to Stan and updated him on what they’d discussed.

“As soon as I hear back from them, I’ll let you know,” Stan assured her.

After saying goodbye, Jessa hung up and pressed a hand to her stomach. Suddenly she felt a bit nervous about everything. It was weird to think about all of them being together under one roof. She was excited, but also a bit worried. He was a stranger. And who knew how Cami would be when she arrived.

“I’ve been wondering,” Violet began, “do you think maybe we should look at renting a couple of RVs?”

Laurel nodded. “I was wondering that too. It will be fine while they’re just doing the west wing, but once they move over to do the east wing, unless we want to double up, there are not going to be enough rooms. Especially now with Will arriving."

"There's no place here to rent anything. We'll have to go to Minneapolis or Fargo." Jessa set her phone on the counter.

"Bemidji might have some rental places, and they're also a bit closer," Laurel suggested. "Or maybe we should ask Lance. He might have some ideas."

Jessa lifted a hand. "I've had my one conversation with Lance today. One of you guys can call him about this."

Violet arched a brow. "You talked to Lance?"

✃ *Chapter Three* ✄

I CALLED to let him know that everything seemed to be on schedule with Cami arriving this week."

"Okay. I'll do the calling around on this one. I need something productive to do anyway," Violet said with a grin.

"I'm going to go and continue to tackle Gran's room," Jessa said, well aware she probably looked less than thrilled at the prospect.

"Do you want my help again?" Laurel asked. "I can come back up after I get supper started."

Jessa shook her head. "You need to take it easy. It's not hard work. It's just...difficult."

Violet nodded. "Would you rather I come help you with that? I can phone about the RVs later."

"No, we need to get that settled." Jessa grabbed a bottle of water from the fridge and made her way upstairs.

Once again in the gloomy room, she sighed. At least the open windows had aired it out enough that none of the musty smell of earlier lingered. Before she started more sorting, Jessa phoned the number Gareth had given her earlier. As she waited for him to answer, she walked to the window and looked out across the backyard to the trees and the lake beyond them.

"Gareth here," he said when he answered the phone.

"Hello, Gareth, this is Jessa."

"I was beginning to think you'd forgotten about me," he said with a laugh.

"Nope. Just having a talk with my sisters."

"Are you going to cancel our dinner plans?" he asked. "I got the feeling they were a little leery of me."

"No, I'm not calling to cancel. I was going to see if you wanted to meet around six." Jessa named a popular restaurant on the south side of town.

"That sounds good. I'll be there," Gareth assured her.

They didn't talk long, and once the call ended, Jessa figured she had about an hour to work. She wanted to leave herself time for a shower to wash away the sweat of the day. Aware that it would eat her battery, but needing the distraction it provided, Jessa set her phone to her favorite playlist and got down to work.

Lance had just walked into his office when his cell phone rang. His frustration over the endless delays and interruptions in his day made him want to ignore the call. He didn't rush to answer it, but waited until he was settled in his chair before responding.

"Lance? This is Violet."

Yet another Collingsworth sister calling him. Not the one he wanted, but he supposed two calls from her in one day would have been too much to hope for. "Hey Violet, what can I do for you?"

"We've been talking here about the possibility of maybe

renting a couple of RVs. It turns out we have at least one more family member coming for the month. And with Matt up here with Laurel, we just figure we need more room, especially once we move from the east wing to the west."

"It's definitely worth considering," Lance agreed. "I had planned to bring one out for my guy who will be there to oversee the project. I think a couple for you ladies might be a good idea."

"Okay, so now that you agree, could you give me an idea of where I might be able to rent them from?"

"Do you want the motor home type or the ones pulled by a truck?"

"That's what we don't know. The pulled ones would probably be cheaper to rent, but we have no way to pull them out here."

"Let me make a few phone calls. I have some friends who have rigs they might not be using until later in the summer. They might rent at a more reasonable rate."

"Thanks, Lance. We appreciate your help with this."

"You're welcome. I'll call you back as soon as I have some information."

"So we're all good to start on Monday?" Violet asked.

"Yep. Jessa called me earlier and said Cami was arriving this week."

"Laurel will be going to Minneapolis to pick her up. Here's hoping for relatively little conflict."

"Cami and Jessa?" Lance guessed.

"Yeah. They didn't get along too well when we were all together for Gran's funeral. That was mainly Cami's fault though. She behaved...badly. I'm hoping the past couple of months have mellowed her out."

"This whole thing is going to be enough of a three-ring circus without adding familial conflicts into the mix," Lance commented.

"Laurel and I will try to keep the peace between them."

"Well, I'll be out there on Friday to do a final walk through and to make sure you all don't have any last minute concerns or questions."

There was a couple of seconds of silence, and Lance wondered if they'd lost their connection.

"Um, I'm just wondering...and I know it might not be any of my business, but I'm going to ask anyway. How do you feel about being around Jessa?"

Lance wasn't quite sure how to answer her question. Frankly, he'd been trying to avoid thinking too much about it. When Julia Collingsworth had first approached him nine months ago about this project, he'd been shocked, to say the least. But she'd insisted he take it and that he'd be well paid for his efforts. In the current economy, how could he say no? Seeing Jessa for the first time in over a decade had given him pause, however. He'd wondered if it really was worth the money though because it had been pretty clear she didn't want to be anywhere around him.

"I think it will be fine," Lance said, well aware he didn't think anything of the sort. "It was a long time ago, and we were both much younger. It's water under the bridge."

Another long pause before Violet said, "I hope you're right. Anyway, like I said, not really my business."

"If I remember correctly what was one sister's business became all the sisters' business," Lance remarked wryly."

"Well, this is true." Violet chuckled. "Thanks for your help with the RVs. Guess we'll see you in a few days."

After their conversation had ended, Lance leaned back in his chair. He needed to approach this in a professional manner. Letting the past interfere would make an intense situation only more difficult. Right now he needed to focus on clearing the last few things off his plate this week so he could give the Collingsworth job the focus it needed. Anything he and Jessa Collingsworth had shared in the past needed to stay there. At least for now.

❧

The teal colored maxi dress Jessa wore whipped against her legs as she walked toward the entrance of the restaurant. She was glad she'd chosen to gather her hair back in a clip otherwise she'd be arriving with a wildly windswept look, thanks to the wind that had kicked up.

Once inside, she spoke to the hostess. At the mention of Gareth's name, the woman nodded and led the way to a small table with two high stools on either side. As they approached, he slid off his seat and smiled.

"Glad to see you didn't change your mind," Gareth said as they sat down across from each other.

Jessa shrugged. "It's been a while since I've been out for dinner. I wouldn't pass this up."

"Ah, so it's not my charming personality and stunning good looks that enticed you," Gareth remarked with a lifted brow and a grin.

Jessa returned his smile as she settled back in her seat. "Actually, it was your interest in gardening that persuaded me to come."

"Hey, I'll take that." Before he could continue, a waitress walked up.

She smiled at Jessa. "Can I get you something to drink?"

"Just water with lemon, thanks."

"And a refill for you?" she asked Gareth.

He nodded. "Thank you."

"Guess we'd better decide what to order before she comes back," Jessa suggested.

It didn't take Jessa much time to choose her meal. Whenever she came to this restaurant, she had the same thing. No sense in ordering something else when she already knew what she liked. It took a bit longer for Gareth to decide and lay his menu down. The waitress showed up shortly after with their drinks and took their order.

Jessa was a bit dismayed to realize that Gareth's refill was actually a beer. If he had any more, she'd have to drive him home, which wasn't something she relished on a first "date." He appeared to drink this one more slowly as they talked. He was an easy person to talk to, especially when they got on the subject of gardening. Their conversation waned a bit when the food arrived, but soon they were once again talking about the large outdoor garden Jessa had on land outside of town.

Aside from the people she'd met back when she was researching the greenhouse, Jessa had never found someone who could speak so knowledgeably about a subject that was important to her. Gareth asked lots of questions and answered any she had about his own experiences with gardening.

They lingered over their meals and even ordered dessert. They had just finished when Gareth's phone rang. He took it out and glanced at the display.

"It's my mum. She'll worry if I don't answer. I'm just going to step outside and chat with her for a minute. I'll be right back."

Jessa nodded with a smile. It was nice to see a son and mom with a good relationship. Gran had always told her you could tell how a guy would treat you by how he treated his mother. Of course, Lance had treated his mother very well and still dumped her, so maybe it wasn't exactly a foolproof theory. As she waited from Gareth to come back, she glanced around the restaurant. It was pretty empty now compared to when they'd arrived. She looked at her phone, surprised to see it was a few minutes past ten already.

"Can I get you anything else?"

Jessa glanced up at the waitress standing next to the table. "I think we're good. Thank you."

Nodding, the woman slid a plastic tray onto the table. "Here's the bill whenever you're ready."

Jessa thanked her again and then spent a little time looking at her phone while she waited for Gareth to return. She glanced at the bill in the tray. Was this officially a date? Or should she be paying for her half? As the minutes ticked by without his return, Jessa glanced around to the door. Maybe she'd just pay for the full bill. After all, he was living on a teacher's salary, and she clearly had more than enough money. She caught the waitress's gaze as she laid her card down on the tray.

She had just finished the transaction with the waitress when Gareth returned.

With an apologetic look, he said, "I'm so sorry. Mum didn't want to stop chatting. I didn't mean for you to get that."

"It's okay," Jessa assured him with a smile.

"At least let me leave a tip," he said as he leaned forward to pull his wallet from his back pocket.

Jessa didn't tell him she'd already added the tip when she paid for the bill. She was just glad he was the type of guy who would leave a tip. Because he hadn't ordered another drink and hadn't even finished his other one from a couple of hours ago, Jessa didn't feel as obliged to offer him a ride home.

"Thank you for a lovely evening," she said to him as they approached her car. She used her fob to unlock the door. "It was a nice break before I get caught up in a bunch of family stuff for the next few weeks."

"I had a nice time too. Maybe we can do it again sometime," he said as he stepped around her to open the door of her car.

"Thanks." Jessa smiled. "Yes, I'd like that."

She slid behind the wheel and tucked her skirt in before Gareth shut the door. After putting the key in, she rolled down her window.

Gareth leaned down. "Drive safe. See you around."

Jessa nodded. "Good night."

He straightened and stepped back from the car when she started it up. As she pulled out of the parking lot onto Main Street, Jessa looked into her rear view mirror and saw his shadowy figure still standing where she'd left him, hands on his hips.

Jessa wasn't in any big rush to get home. No doubt her sisters had questions for her. She might give them a few details, but no way would she mention that she'd picked up the tab for their dinner. Whatever opinion they had of Gareth would drop even lower.

❧ *Chapter Four* ❧

As it turned out, neither sister was downstairs when she arrived. Breathing a sigh of relief, Jessa locked up and turned on the alarm before going upstairs to her room. She took her time getting ready for bed, replaying the evening in her mind. Though it had been a while since she'd been on a date, she had dated over the years. She had even been in a relationship for almost a year. That had come to an end when Aaron, who'd been a youth pastor at the church, decided he felt led to the mission field. Jessa hadn't felt that same calling, so they had ended their relationship, and he'd left Collingsworth to return to his hometown to begin the process of becoming a missionary.

Jessa's hairbrush strokes slowed as her memories of that time surfaced. She had thought she loved him, and Gran had liked him. But on the night they mutually agreed to go their separate ways, she hadn't felt the devastated heartbreak she remembered from when things with Lance had ended. She'd realized then that the hurt she'd felt over Lance had been enough to keep her from fully investing her heart in any future relationship.

The agony of the breakup with Lance hadn't just resulted

from the ending of the relationship. That had been hard enough, but the twisting of the knife had come when she'd heard he had gotten engaged just two weeks later, and that the woman he was engaged to was pregnant. Now she hadn't known a lot about pregnancy back then, but she knew enough to realize that for her to be pregnant enough for people to know, he had to have been with the girl before they even officially broke up. That...that was what had hurt more than anything else and was what she was determined never to feel again.

Setting her brush down, Jessa turned from the mirror and went to her bed. It was going to be hard not to dwell on the past during the renovations with Lance around, but she was determined to knuckle through it. He wouldn't know how much he had hurt her. She would never give him that satisfaction.

Jessa got up early the next morning to tackle Gran's room some more. Laurel planned to leave around noon, so Jessa wanted to have as much done as possible to send with her to the thrift shop. At the very least, she wanted all the clothes gone. She still had to sort through her bookcases, nightstands and desk, but Jessa didn't think those contained much that would be suitable for donation.

She and Violet managed to cram all of the black garbage bags filled with clothes into Laurel's car. Jessa went ahead and added the box of toiletries that none of them wanted. As she watched Laurel drive off, she felt a bit of weight lift from her shoulders. Still lots to do, but that had been a big step.

After dropping Rose off at her birthday party sleepover, Jessa returned to continue working on Gran's room. Violet had offered her help, so Jessa had set her to work gathering up all the paintings, pictures and other knickknacks in the hallways and rooms. They were things they'd put in the portable storage unit scheduled for delivery that afternoon.

"Did I tell you Lance will be coming by later to drop off an RV?" Violet asked as she stepped into the sitting room of

Gran's suite.

Jessa looked up from the books she was placing in the box on the floor. "Um, no. Why is he dropping off an RV?"

"When I called him about it the other day, he said he'd call a few friends who had RVs who might be willing to rent them at an affordable rate to us for the month."

"So he found one?" Jessa turned back to pull more books from the case, her stomach suddenly in knots.

"Actually, he found two. He's dropping one off today and then will bring the other one on Friday when he comes out again."

"That was nice of him." Jessa fought to keep her tone even as she added more books to the box. She'd been trying not to think about how much she'd have to interact with Lance in the days ahead.

"I thought so. He saved me having to figure out not just where to get the RVs from, but how to get them out here." Violet walked over to the bookcase where Jessa was working. "Haven't stumbled across any more secrets, have you?"

Jessa glanced over at her and shook her head. "I haven't been looking too closely at the stuff I'm packing away, but I figure if she wanted us to find something else, it would jump out at us like the one did with Laurel."

"True," Violet agreed. "I'm checking the backs of paintings and pictures to make sure she didn't tape anything to them."

Jessa let out a laugh. "You think she'd do something like that?"

Violet shrugged. "Who knows. With what we've learned already, nothing would surprise me."

The melodic chimes of the doorbell had them both turning toward the door leading to the master bedroom. Jessa set down the books she held in her hand and led the way out of the sitting room to the bedroom and out into the hall.

"Jessa!" Lily called up the stairs. "Someone's here to drop off a bin or something?"

Jessa jogged down the hallway to the top of the staircase. As she neared the bottom, she saw the door standing open with Lily beside it. A large man stood there, a clipboard in his hand.

"Hi," Jessa greeted him as she approached him.

He looked down at the clipboard. "We're here to drop off a storage bin for the Collingsworths."

"That's us." Jessa stepped out onto the front porch, blinking a bit at the bright sunlight. "If possible, I'd like it to go right next to the garage."

The man looked to where she pointed and nodded. "We should be able to put it there, no problem."

He returned to the large truck that sat rumbling in the driveway. Jessa, Lily and Violet watched as the man drove the truck the opposite way around the circular driveway so that the back of the truck was lined up with the spot where Jessa wanted it. A second man jumped out and stood at the back of the driver side to help guide him into place.

It didn't take too long to get it situated. After it was positioned correctly, the man returned to have her sign a form and then drove the truck back down the driveway. The reality of what lay ahead was slowly sinking in.

They hadn't even moved off the porch when the rumble of another engine caught their attention. Lifting a hand to shade her eyes, Jessa watched as a large black truck came into view pulling a trailer.

"Looks like Lance is here with the first RV," Violet said as she stepped past Jessa. She waved as the truck drew closer.

It came to a stop in front of the house, and the silence of the afternoon seemed overwhelming when the engine of the vehicle turned off.

Lance rounded the front of the truck while another man climbed out of the passenger seat.

"Hello, ladies," Lance said with a smile. "Brought you a home on wheels."

"Thanks," Violet said as she walked down the steps to meet them. "Looks great!"

"This is my cousin, Josh." Lance motioned to the lanky man who stood next to him. "He's going to be the project manager for this job. I'll be here a lot, but if I'm not around, he'll be the guy in charge. Josh, this is Jessa, Violet and...Lily?"

"Yep," Violet confirmed. "It's nice to meet you, Josh." She held out a hand to him. As he shook it, she asked, "Has Lance warned you about us all yet?"

Josh glanced toward Lance as he released Violet's hand. Jessa also shook his hand, as did Lily, who then disappeared into the house.

Lance grinned. "Hey, I can't send a guy into a situation loaded with women without some warning, can I?"

"Would have loved to have been a fly on the wall for that conversation," Violet said and laughed.

Jessa wished she was as at ease in Lance's presence, but right then, all she wanted was for him to leave. But instead he turned his gaze to her and smiled. "So, where do you want this thing parked?"

Crossing her arms over her waist, Jessa glanced to where the storage bin had just been positioned. "I'm assuming they need to be out of the way of other vehicles that might be coming to deliver things. I think around the side would be the best."

Lance looked to where she motioned and then said, "Walk with me. Let's check it out."

Jessa shot Violet a look. Violet gave a barely perceptible nod which Jessa hoped meant that she wasn't going to leave her alone with Lance. Moving slowly, she walked to the steps and made her way down them to where Lance stood. He fell into step beside her as they headed along the paved single lane road that ran between the garage and the house. It led to her greenhouse if followed right to its end, but as they approached the spot where the road disappeared into the trees, Jessa stopped.

"I would like to have them parked here." Jessa gestured to the spot along the tree line where the yard ended and the heavily wooded area began.

Jessa watched as Lance surveyed where she'd gestured. He turned to Josh as he and Violet joined them. "What do you think?"

The two men moved off the paved road and walked along the tree line. Jessa could hear them talking but couldn't make out what they were saying. She moved closer with Violet on her heels.

Lance smiled as they came to where he and Josh stood. "I think it will work. The ground is pretty level. We're going to have three in total."

"Three?" Jessa asked. "I thought Violet just said you were getting two."

"Yes, for you ladies. I was planning to bring mine along for Josh and me."

Jessa nodded her understanding though the thought of having Lance close night and day was more than a little disconcerting. "That makes sense."

"We'll bring the other one on Friday when we come to do a final walk through, and then I'll bring mine on Monday." Lance turned his gaze back to Jessa. "How are things coming inside? Will you be ready for us by Monday?"

"Yes. We're working hard on Gran's suite already. Once those are all cleared out, we'll move on to the other rooms. The storage bin arrived earlier, so we're good to go."

"Are you going to need help moving the furniture?"

"I think we'll be okay. Matt is coming on Friday, and Dean will most likely be available to give us a hand too."

Violet nodded. "And he could probably get a couple of guys from the station to help as well if we need it."

"That's good," Lance said. "Well, let's get this first machine in place."

Josh stayed behind as they walked back to the front of the house. Jessa stood with Violet and watched as Lance drove the truck down the road and around the corner of the house. No sooner had the truck begun to position the trailer when the sound of another vehicle approaching drew their attention.

"Grand central station around here today," Violet commented as they both looked toward the bend in the driveway.

Jessa didn't immediately recognize the vehicle that slowly drove into view. It came to a stop where the truck had been parked just minutes earlier. It was an older model two door sporty looking car. When the door opened, and the driver got out, Jessa felt her stomach knot. *Gareth.*

Jessa heard Violet mutter under her breath, but couldn't make out what she said. She tossed a *behave yourself* look at Violet before she turned her attention to the man heading their way.

He gave a wave as he came around the front of the car.

"Hi, Gareth," Jessa said as he drew near. "I didn't expect to see you today."

An easy smile crossed his face. "I didn't have a class this afternoon, and it was too nice a day to spend inside grading papers. Thought I'd stop by and see what you were doing." He looked over to where the truck had backed in with the trailer. "Looks like you have some activity going on here."

Jessa explained the plan to Gareth. "That's the first of three that we'll have here."

Lance jumped out of the driver's side and walked toward the trailer which took him out of view from where they stood. Jessa found herself wishing that Gareth would leave before

Lance finished, and then couldn't figure out why she felt that way. It shouldn't matter if the two of them met, but for some reason, it did. Unfortunately, Gareth showed no sign of leaving and happily chatted with her and Violet.

"I guess you're going to be pretty busy for the next little while," Gareth commented after asking about the renovation plans.

Before Jessa could reply, she heard male voices coming from behind her and glanced over her shoulder to see Lance and Josh approaching. The truck sat parked on the roadway, unhitched from the trailer. Lance came to a stop, hands on hips, looking at Gareth. Trying to hide how awkward it was for her, Jessa introduced them.

"Gareth, this is Lance Evanston and his cousin, Josh. They're here to do work on the house for the next few weeks." Gesturing to Gareth, Jessa continued, "This is Gareth Williams. He's a professor at the college. He has an interest in gardening like I do."

Gareth didn't respond at first, but then he smiled and held out his hand. "Nice to meet you, mate."

First Josh shook his hand, then Lance, who also said, "Nice to meet you too."

When neither man said anything further, Gareth turned back to Jessa and said, "I enjoyed our dinner last night. I hope we can do it again sometime."

Jessa nodded, acutely aware of Lance standing near her. "Yes, I enjoyed it too."

Seeing the two men together like this, their differences were marked. Gareth's easygoing posture and smile were in direct contrast to Lance's rigid stance and expression. Though they were close to the same height, Gareth was more lean and lanky than Lance. And his blond hair hung in long, loose curls where Lance's black hair was cut short and worn more stylishly.

Jessa gave herself a shake. Why was she comparing

them? This was not a competition. Lance had moved on. So had she. Though she wouldn't say that Gareth was her future, he certainly was a more likely candidate than Lance.

"Well, I guess you're doing business here, so I'll leave you to it," Gareth said.

Jessa moved to his side and walked around to the driver's side door with him, her back to Lance. "Sorry about this. There are a lot of last minute details to take care of before we start work on Monday."

Gareth's gaze went past her to where the men stood with Violet. "He doesn't look too happy to see me." His green gaze came back to hers. "Is there something I should know?"

Jessa shoved a chunk of hair behind her ear. "We had a thing many years ago. It's been long over."

"Really? He seems to think otherwise."

"He shouldn't." Jessa shrugged, keeping her voice low as she said, "I just met him again a couple of weeks ago for the first time in over ten years. Whatever we had as teenagers is long over."

Gareth smiled. "If you say so. Give me a call when you're free for dinner or maybe some gardening."

"I will. No promises how soon it might be though. A lot depends on the work here."

"Well, if I can help out in any way, let me know."

Jessa smiled. "I will."

Gareth gave her a wink and then leaned close to brush his lips to her cheek. "Just giving him something to think about."

Normally Jessa would have protested, but instead she managed a stilted laugh. Crossing her arms over her waist, she stepped back to allow room for Gareth to maneuver his car around the circular drive. She was a little upset by the developments of the past few minutes. Not because of what Gareth had done in kissing her the way he had, but because his closeness had stirred nothing in her. She'd felt more attraction to Aaron.

Clearly, even though she didn't want to admit it, she did have a type and apparently it wasn't Gareth. Disappointed in herself for even feeling that way, Jessa let out a quick breath and tried to relax her expression before returning to where the other three stood.

When she met Violet's gaze, her sister just lifted a brow before saying, "Lance says the bin for all the demo garbage will be here first thing Monday morning."

Though she didn't want to, Jessa looked at Lance and nodded. "That sounds good."

His expression was hard to read, but she knew she couldn't allow herself to care about what he thought since, from all indications, he was in a relationship if not married. He wore no ring, but she knew that guys often didn't. Regardless, he had no right to care or have an opinion about anything she did with her life now.

"Well, we should head out," Josh said. He shifted from one foot to the other, his gaze on his cousin. "We promised Daphne we'd be back before supper."

❧ Chapter Five ❧

LANCE glanced at Josh and then gave a quick nod of his head. "We'll see you guys on Friday when we drop off the other trailer. And if it's convenient, I'd like to take a final walk through then just to make sure we all know what's going on. Will that work?"

"That will be fine," Jessa told him.

"Okay. See you Friday then."

As the two men walked toward the big black truck, Josh tossed a set of keys in Lance's direction. He quickly snagged them out of the air and opened the driver's door and swung himself up into the seat. The engine roared to life, and Lance gave them a wave out the open window as he drove away.

"Well," Violet said. "That was...weird."

"I hope that's the last of the visitors for the day," Jessa said as she headed for the stairs. Inside the house, she went to the kitchen and got a bottle of cold water from the fridge. When Violet came in, before she could open her mouth, Jessa told her, "Don't even say anything."

Violet wrinkled her nose. "You mean you don't want to

talk about the terribly awkward situation of having a new guy you barely know kiss you in front of your old boyfriend?"

"My old married boyfriend." Jessa took a sip of water and recapped the bottle.

"You don't know that he's married," Violet pointed out. "He doesn't wear a ring. He hasn't mentioned a wife."

"Last I heard, he was engaged to be married."

"Engaged to be married is a lot different from being married. Lots could have happened between now and then," Violet said. "I think I should just ask him. That would get rid of that particular argument you keep throwing out there."

Jessa set her water bottle on the counter and picked at the label on it. "Listen, it doesn't matter if he's married or not. There can never be anything between us again. It just can't happen."

Violet settled herself on a stool across the counter from where Jessa stood. "Why? You've never talked much about what went down with Gran and Lance back then. If it had just been Gran that separated you two, then, provided he isn't married, there's no reason to not consider that maybe something might work."

"It won't happen." Jessa sighed. "I don't know what Gran was thinking back then, or why she hired him for this job now, but I'm not going to get caught up in it. He's here to do a job. We have a part to play in it, but that's all it's going to be."

Violet shook her head. "You can try to control all this as much as you want, but sometimes, you just can't control how you feel. I sincerely doubt Gran would have hired Lance if he were married. There's something else going on here, and the sooner you get it figured out, the better."

Unwilling to continue discussing the subject, Jessa said, "I'm going to keep working on Gran's stuff. Do you have things ready to bring down to the storage unit?"

"I do, but I'm not sure if we should put smaller stuff in

first or the larger furniture."

"I'm a bit concerned we're not going to have enough space, but I guess we do have all the room in the garage as well. We don't need to park any cars in there for the time being."

Once Jessa saw what all needed to be moved, she and Violet conscripted Lily to help them take it down to the garage. They raided the linen closet and used sheets to wrap and cover the more precious items to hopefully keep them from any damage. It wasn't the ideal way to store things, but since it was temporary, Jessa hoped it would work.

༺◦✍༒

Lance gripped the wheel tightly as the truck hurdled its way towards Fargo. He knew he shouldn't be upset by what had transpired at the manor. He had no right to be, but that didn't mean he could shake the urge to strangle Mr. Hippy. It wasn't until the moment when he'd realized that the man and Jessa had some sort of relationship, did Lance discover that even though he'd tried to deny it, there was a small part of him that had hoped there might be a chance to revive the past.

"That was...uh...interesting," Josh commented after almost half an hour of silence.

Lance shot him a look. "Yeah, just a bit."

"And there are two more sisters?" Josh asked.

"Yep. Laurel and Cami. I think Violet said Laurel was in Minneapolis picking Cami up, so you'll meet them on Friday. They're a unique bunch of women; that's for sure."

"Jess and Violet don't seem very similar," Josh said.

"They aren't. From what I remember, each of them is unique. Violet and Laurel are probably the most alike. Julia Collingsworth definitely had her hands full with the four of them."

Silence filled the cab of the truck for a few minutes, a little more weighted this time. Finally, Josh asked, "Did you love her?"

Lance glanced at Josh. They had grown close over the past six years. Though cousins, they hadn't been together a lot growing up since his family had lived in Collingsworth, and Josh's had lived overseas as missionaries. But when Josh's life had fallen apart seven years earlier, Lance had offered him a place to stay. And as they'd gotten to know each other, they'd become best friends. If there were anyone he could be totally honest with, it would be Josh.

"Yes. Back then she was shy, but lots of people thought she was a snob because of the family money and name. She told me once the reason she didn't hang out with kids her age was that she didn't know who was a true friend and who just wanted to be her friend because of who she was. I think that was true of most the sisters." Though they talked about a lot of stuff, Jessa was a subject Lance had never brought up. It had never seemed relevant until recently.

"How did you get her to trust you?"

"Each of the sisters had to do something in the way of a job, even though they weren't paid. One of the things Jessa did was to tutor other kids in things like literature and writing. I did fine with math and science, but my English classes were torture. Usually Jessa helped younger kids, but agreed to take me on in preparation for my SATs. The rest, as they say, is history."

"Why did you end things?"

"I had no choice. Julia Collingsworth told me that it was in my best interests to end things with Jessa."

"And that was that? You didn't try to fight for her?" Josh asked.

Lance sighed. "Mom had just gotten sick, and Dad was getting ready to move us all to Fargo for his new job. Julia knew that money was an issue, particularly with Mom's medicine and bills for the things insurance didn't cover. And she was most insistent that it couldn't work between Jessa and me." Lance frowned at the memory. Julia had been almost frantic to end things between them. "I knew that what Julia Collingsworth wanted, Julia Collingsworth got. If I didn't agree to break up with Jessa then, it would happen eventually. She would make sure of that. So I took the money she offered and left."

"Wow, I never realized..."

"Then everything happened with Daphne, and there was no going back after that."

"Why on earth, after all that, would she come to you to work alongside Jessa again?"

Lance shook his head. "Your guess is as good as mine. I wish I knew. When I asked her, she just said that she felt she owed me and would make it worth my while. And frankly, in this economic environment, I would have been a fool to turn it down."

"True. I just hope that the overall cost isn't higher than you can afford to pay."

Lance hoped the same thing. Julia had as much as come right out and said that Jessa was still single. Obviously Mr. Hippy had been a development after the older woman's passing. He had to admit that knowing she wasn't married had played a role in his decision to take the job, though money had still been a big part as well.

As he thought about the situation, he acknowledged for the first time that he had not really prayed about this on. Usually he took the time to pray before bidding on or accepting an offer. He had seen this job as a possible answer to two prayers, not necessarily as something he needed to pray about. On the business side of things, for the past year he'd prayed for a large job to come in so he could build more of a financial cushion for the company. And on the personal side, he'd been praying daily for a wife. Past thirty now, he wanted to settle down and start a family. He'd had a couple of serious relationships over the years, but nothing had worked out. So he continued to pray.

When Julia Collingsworth had approached him with this job, he saw the definite answer to one prayer, and the possible answer to another. Jessa had been the love of his youth, and still she lingered in his heart all these years later. He'd hoped that perhaps there was still something there, but this latest twist of events made him reconsider. Maybe this job hadn't been God's will after all. Or maybe it was, but not in the way he had thought. Either way, he'd certainly be praying about all aspects of it in the days ahead.

"I guess time will tell. If things get too difficult, I know I can trust you to run things while I'm not around."

"I'll do my best. You can get through this," Josh assured him.

Lance hoped his cousin was right. If anyone knew about surviving difficult times in life, it was Josh. His cousin had his utmost respect for how he'd dealt with the blows life had handed him. He'd survived, and so could Lance. Because this was nothing compared to what Josh had endured. He just needed to man up, do the job and let the chips fall where they may.

~∞~

In the quiet of the night, Jessa moved through Gran's rooms once again. The sitting room was completely devoid of all but the furniture. All the books, knickknacks and pictures had been packed away and taken to the garage. The closet and chest of drawers were empty. Slowly but surely, Gran's life was being packed away.

Jessa pulled her arms tight across her chest. The rooms, though emptied of Gran's things, still seemed to be filled with her presence. It was an eerie feeling. Almost as if Gran was watching over her shoulder as she picked through her things. But it was important that she be the one to do this most intimate of tasks for Gran.

Dean had stopped by with supper and then helped them move some of the lighter furniture downstairs. The heavier stuff would have to wait for Matt and maybe a couple more guys to help out. Now Violet and Lily were in their rooms, so it was just Jessa, her thoughts and Gran's stuff.

Moving slowly, Jessa walked to the bed and sank down on its uncovered mattress. She reached for the handle of the nightstand. In the back of her mind was the thought of more secrets to come. When she'd finished packing up Gran's desk earlier, Jessa had breathed a sigh of relief that there had been nothing more hidden there. But that didn't mean they were in the clear yet.

She opened the drawer and stared at the books and papers stashed inside. For some reason, her stomach knotted as she reached to pull out the contents. Without looking at it, she emptied the entire drawer onto the mattress.

With a quick sigh, Jessa turned to settle on the bed so she could sort through it and place what needed to be kept in the box at her elbow. Slowly she worked her way through receipts, bills and papers that held no important information. Finally, she reached the last of the contents she'd spilled onto the bed. A large leather bound Bible. Jessa wanted to just shove it into the box with the rest of the stuff, but instead she settled it on her lap and allowed it to fall open.

Immediately it revealed an envelope. Jessa gritted her teeth and turned her head. She blew out a long breath before looking back, knowing her hope that it would be gone was futile. And indeed it was. Another envelope that matched the one Laurel had found lay there. Jessa removed it from the Bible and laid it on the bed. She put the Bible in the box after a quick check that nothing else lay within its pages.

The irony of finding another letter hidden within the pages of truth did not escape Jessa. While Gran had not been outspoken about her faith, it was only after her death and the revelation of secrets that Jessa had begun to question if Gran had ever fully embraced God. It didn't seem she left anything up to Him. She was too busy trying to make sure everything worked out the way she wanted for the protection and betterment of the Collingsworth name.

Ignoring the envelope for the time being, Jessa closed up the box and took it into the hallway. She stood there for a moment, wishing for all the world she could just avoid what was undoubtedly one more secret that none of them wanted to know. She returned to the room with another box and emptied the other night stand of its contents. Thankfully, nothing else jumped out at her.

She cleared the last few things off Gran's dresser and the other end table that sat beside the large chair near the window. When the box was full, it joined the other in the hallway. Knowing there was nothing else she could do in the room, Jessa reluctantly retrieved the envelope and left the room, plunging it into darkness as she stepped into the hallway.

With a glance toward Violet's door, Jessa slipped into her room. She put the envelope on her desk and went to take a shower. The day of moving stuff around had left her feeling dirty and hot. After the shower, she pulled on a pair of shorts and t-shirt and went downstairs. As she unloaded the dishwasher that had been run earlier, Jessa tried to think of anything but the letter waiting upstairs.

As she wiped down the counters, she thought about Cami's arrival the next day. After her last visit, Jessa could only imagine how this one was going to go. She was resolved to do her part to avoid conflict with her, but she really couldn't stand the stupidity of some of the things her younger sister did. The incident before Gran's funeral was still too fresh in her memory for her to dismiss it as something Cami wouldn't do again. But she could always hope.

Her phone rang as she was hanging up the dishtowel. She plucked it off the counter, surprised to see Stan's number on the screen.

"Hi, Stan," she said.

"I hope I'm not calling too late," Stan replied.

"No problem. I'm still up."

"Getting ready for the big renovation?" he asked.

"Yeah. Lots to get moved out before they start the demo on Monday. We're making progress though, so I'm hoping it will be all ready to go."

"Well, I'm calling because I finally heard back from William."

Jessa realized that was something else she'd been trying to avoid thinking about. "Is he going to be able to make it?"

"Yes. He's flying in Friday afternoon. There was no way he could make it in time to come back with Laurel since you said she'd be picking Cami up tomorrow. But I'm hoping that he might still be able to hitch a ride with Matt."

"That should be okay."

"He's supposed to arrive around 5:20 Friday afternoon."

"I'll text Laurel to let her know. Hopefully, that will work with Matt's schedule. I know he sometimes works late."

"Will said he'd be willing to wait around the airport if necessary. I'll give you his number to pass on to Matt so they can talk about meeting up."

Jessa scribbled down the number he rattled off to her as well as the flight information. "Thanks so much, Stan. Appreciate you helping out with this."

There was a pause and then Stan said, "How are you doing?"

Jessa thought of the envelope on her desk upstairs. "I'm doing okay. It's a lot to take in. Gran should have dealt with this while she was alive. It's not fair that we have to process all of this without her here."

"Yes, I agree, but I also think perhaps it is a little easier without her around. You can allow yourself to experience your true feelings about all of this."

"Sort of. Though it doesn't feel right to be angry at a dead person," Jessa comment ruefully.

"I honestly think your gran would understand. Just don't hold it all in like she did," Stan cautioned. "Well, I'm going to let you go. If you have any questions, be sure to let me know."

After hanging up, Jessa thought about calling Laurel but decided not to interrupt her evening with Matt. They deserved some time together after all they'd been through. Instead, she sent a text with Will's flight information and phone number and told Laurel to call her the next day.

Back upstairs she finished getting ready for bed and crawled between the sheets. Jessa checked one last time for a text from Laurel before setting her phone on the nightstand and snapping off the lamp. In the darkness of the room, she curled onto her side and let out a long sigh. For the first time all day she felt the tension ease from her body. This was her time of day. No one was asking her to do anything. There was nothing demanding her attention. It was just her and her thoughts.

And the envelope.

Jessa turned to her other side and grabbed another pillow, pulling it close. She resolutely closed her eyes and willed sleep to come. Unfortunately, it was more elusive than ever.

No more secrets. Was it really too much to ask? She didn't want to have to deal with any more secrets.

Back over to her other side, dragging the pillow with her. *Sleep. Sleep. Sleep.*

Finally, Jessa tossed aside her covers and swung her feet over the edge of the bed to sit up. Irritation flowed through her. Mainly it was directed at Gran, but she was also irritated with herself for not just dealing with whatever was in the envelope. With a flick of her fingers, she turned the lamp back on before she stood and walked to the desk to retrieve the dreaded holder of secrets.

She returned to the bed and plunked herself back against the pillows. After taking another deep breath, she ran her finger under the flap to break the seal. Inside the larger envelope were two smaller ones. One was addressed to her. The other said, in bold black pen, "When you are ready to learn about your mother."

Not if...*when*.

She knew for Violet, that time was already at hand. For herself, however, Jessa wasn't sure she was ready to hear about their mother. She would make a decision on that envelope later, so Jessa set it aside and focused on the one bearing her name.

❧ *Chapter Six* ❧

NOW that she'd made the decision to see what secrets the envelope held, Jessa didn't hesitate to open the one addressed to her. She unfolded the papers it held and began to read her grandmother's familiar script.

My darling Jessamine,

I have put off writing this letter as long as I could. The guilt I feel for what I did to you is more than you'll ever know. To do to you what was done to me, when I knew the pain it caused me is unforgivable. All I can say in my defense is that I thought I was doing the right thing at the time. Now that I've found out I was wrong, I am trying to do what I can to correct the situation.

From the moment your mother got pregnant with you, she told me your father was George Evanston.

Jessa felt her stomach roll at the sight of the name. She looked away from the letter to stare blankly at the wall. *Lance's uncle.* Even without reading further, pieces of the puzzle fell into place. Swallowing hard, Jessa looked back down at the letter, almost scared to read on.

There were plenty of rumors of George's behavior floating around. He was so much younger than Lance's father and nowhere near the man Buck Evanston was. If what your mother told me was true, it meant you and Lance were cousins. I went to George and demanded the truth, but he denied it. All I could think was that of course he would. He could have been charged with rape because of his age and your mother's. When I found out that you were getting serious with Lance, I knew I couldn't allow things to continue between you. I couldn't take the chance that George was actually telling the truth.

When I asked you about your mother late last year, I was surprised when you told me that she had revealed who your father was. I was even more surprised— shocked really—when the name you gave me wasn't George Evanston. I decided it was time to get to the bottom of it all. I couldn't find the man your mother had told you was your father, but I was able to track down George. This time around I demanded he back up his denials with a paternity test. When he readily agreed, I knew I'd made a terrible mistake. The test results confirmed that. George Evanston wasn't your father.

I had had such hopes for you and Aaron, but when that ended, and you never seemed terribly interested in anyone else, I felt like history was repeating itself. Was Lance your one true love in the way that Les, Dean's grandfather, had been mine? I didn't want you to live a life without love the way I did. I loved your grandfather, but sadly, never the way I'd loved Les.

From George, I was able to find Lance. When I discovered that he was currently not in a relationship, I decided to do what I could to bring you two back together. It was just a fortunate stroke of luck that he was in an occupation I could make use of. I hope as you two work together, there might still be something there of the love you once shared. If not, at least I've gone to my grave knowing that I did try to make amends for what I did.

I hope you will forgive me, darling. I thought I was doing the right thing. I know I didn't say it enough, but I love you. Never doubt that. Everything I ever did was out of love for you and your sisters and to protect each of you.

The words on the paper blurred as Jessa stared at them. Her heart felt like it had just been flayed wide open. All those years lost. She wanted to be angry at Gran, but in reality, she had to acknowledge that things would have ended regardless. A pregnancy and the subsequent engagement would have guaranteed that. Apparently he was now divorced, but while what Gran had done had hurt; it was Lance's action following that which had really and truly ripped her heart to shreds.

Unfortunately, Jessa was pretty sure Gran hadn't known about that part. The last thing Jessa had wanted to hear back then was "*I told you so,*" so she had never told Gran that she'd heard Lance had gotten engaged shortly after they broke things off. And that the girl he was engaged to was pregnant. She'd never heard if they had actually gotten married because Lance's family had moved away soon after she'd heard the news.

So now Gran had brought the man back into her life, but it wouldn't make any difference. In the end, he was the one who had completely broken her heart. Gran had hurt and angered her, but Lance had made sure that things were well and truly over between them.

Jessa crumpled the letter in her hands. She swiped angrily at the hot tears that slid down her cheeks. She had shed too many tears over Lance. He would not be allowed to hurt her again. She would get through this renovation and welcome his departure from her life once more. He was not the long lost love Gran had thought. He was the one that she'd been fortunate to escape.

Anger dried her tears as Jessa shoved the letter along with the other unopened envelope into the drawer of her nightstand. Unfortunately, the emotional turmoil in her mind made sleep even more elusive. Opening the envelope hadn't given her the peace she needed. But finally, after seeing the glowing numbers on her clock flip over to 2:00, she fell asleep.

Morning came early, and although Jessa would have loved to stay in bed, there was too much to do for her to lounge around. Feeling sluggish from lack of sleep, Jessa took another shower in hopes that it would invigorate her. While it didn't completely do the job, it did help clear some of the cobwebs from her head.

Dressed in jean capris and a plain T-shirt, Jessa gathered her curls back in a ponytail and skipped the makeup altogether. There was a lot to do that day, and none of it involved impressing anyone. Before she left her room, she checked her phone and saw there was a text from Laurel. She said she'd passed on the information to Matt, and he would take care of getting Will out to Collingsworth. Another text following that one said she and Cami should be back out to the manor by two.

Not all too thrilled at the prospect of Cami's arrival, Jessa said a prayer for patience as she dealt with her again. Downstairs in the kitchen, Jessa found Violet already there making coffee.

"Morning," Jessa said as she pulled a yogurt from the fridge. "Lily up yet?"

"Not that I've seen. You're probably gonna need dynamite to get that girl out of bed this early," Violet replied as she poured coffee into two mugs. As she handed one to Jessa, her brows rose. "Bad night?"

Maybe a little makeup would have been beneficial, but it was too late now. "Yeah, didn't get as much sleep as usual, plus skipped my makeup, so all my flaws are out for the world to see."

Violet laughed. "Flaws? I dare say that flaws would never dare to show themselves on your body."

Jessa glared at her over the rim of her coffee cup. "For that comment, you get to rouse our youngest sibling."

"Aw. Shoulda kept my mouth shut."

"Indeed," Jessa said with a grin. "By the way, Stan called me last night."

After Jessa had given her the condensed version of the conversation along with the reply from Laurel, Violet said, "So weird to think of meeting a brother at this age."

Jessa nodded. "At least he's had most his life to get used to the idea."

They fell silent as Jessa began to eat her toast. Violet got up to refill her cup of coffee, and as she settled back down at the counter, she asked, "You ready for Cami?"

"Just need to put sheets on the bed," Jessa replied, knowing full well the look she'd get from Violet at that comment.

Her sister didn't fail her. Violet rolled her eyes and gave her head a shake. "Seriously?"

Jessa sighed. "I'm as ready as I'll ever be. I'm just hoping she's coming back with a little more maturity. I can't handle too many of those incidents like the one in the bar."

Violet nodded. "I'm in agreement with you on that one. Pretty sure Dean would rather she stay out of trouble too. He can't keep her out of hot water every time she pulls a stunt like that without it smacking of favoritism."

"Let him know he has my permission to deal with Cami as he would anyone if she starts pulling stunts like last time."

"I've said as much to him already," Violet replied. "Maybe if she realizes she's not going to get special treatment, she'll think twice before doing anything stupid."

Jessa gave a humorless laugh. "Yeah, somehow I don't think getting special treatment even crossed her alcohol saturated brain that night."

Once finished with their breakfast, Violet offered to clean

up while Jessa went to finish prepping Cami's room. She'd stripped the bed after Matt had spent that one night there. Now she worked quickly to put the clean sheets on the bed and opened the window to let in some fresh air. There was nothing that showed this room had been Cami's at one time. Anything she had decorated with as a teen was long gone.

As she smoothed the comforter into place, Jessa took a moment to pray for her sister and her own attitude toward her. From very young, they had conflicted. It had been hard because they were so different. Jessa had been the older, more responsible one while Cami had seemed to get into trouble at every turn and never seemed to care about it. Gran had struggled with it, and now Jessa was in the same position. But she really didn't want to alienate her the way Gran had though Jessa knew that hadn't been the older woman's intention.

Once done in Cami's room, Jessa joined Violet and Lily, who had reluctantly left her bed, and they began to move anything small enough for them to handle from the upper rooms. Jessa figured they'd all start sleeping in the RVs on Sunday night so they could remove the rest of the furniture from the bedrooms over the weekend. She was fairly certain the demo would be easier and quicker if the entire upstairs was empty, even though Lance hadn't specifically asked for it. Not that she was trying to speed the process along or anything.

"Do you remember from the plans if we need to empty the library?" Jessa asked Violet as they maneuvered a small end table down the stairs.

"I'm thinking no, but can't say for sure."

"Maybe you could phone Lance to ask," Jessa suggested.

Violet let down her side of the end table as they reached the main floor. "Maybe you could."

Jessa glared at her. "I'll just ask him on Friday."

"Chicken." Violet lifted her side and gave Jessa a pointed look.

Without responding, Jessa picked up the other side, and they carried it out to the garage. It should be enough that he was a part of her romantic past for Violet to understand why she didn't want to have any more contact with Lance than absolutely necessary. However, it didn't seem to be. And Jessa wasn't going to give her any more information about what had gone on back then.

As they walked up the steps of the manor, Violet pulled her phone from her pocket. "I'll give him a call."

"Thank you," Jessa said, holding open the front door for Violet. She followed her into the kitchen and got them both something to drink while Violet placed the call.

"Hey, Lance. It's Violet." She paused a bit then said, "Yep, everything is going good. Jessa was just wondering what the plans were for the library. We couldn't remember."

Jessa wished she'd asked Violet to put it on speaker so she could hear too.

"So just redoing the windows and flooring? Could we protect the bookcases with plastic or do we need to empty them completely?"

Lily walked into the kitchen and frowned. "I thought we were working on the rest of the stuff in that room."

Jessa pointed to Violet. "She's just phoned Lance to ask a couple questions. You can take a break while we wait."

Lily nodded and went to the fridge. "Are you going to need me all day?"

The young girl's reluctance to help out frustrated Jessa a little. She was supposed to be helping out just like all the sisters were. She had a feeling she'd already be fighting to get Cami to work; she didn't need the same attitude from Lily. "I want to get through at least the two rooms up there. Then we'll have to pack up our own rooms and move things down. If you'd rather just work on packing up your own stuff, that's fine."

Lily nodded. "I'd rather do that. Can I just use the boxes

up there?"

"Yes, but this doesn't mean you get out of helping with the other stuff too. We need all hands on deck to get this done before the crew arrives on Monday. And I'll need you to go get Rose around eleven. Can you do that for me?"

"Yep. I can do that." Taking her bottle of water with her, Lily left the kitchen just as Violet hung up.

Having missed the last part of their exchange, Jessa listened as Violet explained what Lance had told her.

"He said the windows and the flooring are the major things, but that the walls will have to be painted after they've installed the new windows. Plastic sheeting can protect the bookcases if we use it to cover them. He'll have some of his guys help us with that."

"That will be better than trying to pack up everything in there," Jessa said.

"Oh, he did say one other thing," Violet said as she picked up her bottle of water.

"What's that?"

"If you have any more questions, feel free to call him." Violet gave her a wide grin before leaving the kitchen.

Jessa fought the urge to toss her water bottle at her sister's back. Instead, she gripped it tightly and followed Violet up the stairs.

They stopped for lunch when Lily got home with Rose. Afterward , the young girl willingly helped Violet and Jessa with whatever they told her to do, while Lily closed herself off in her room. Jessa just hoped it was more packing than texting, but with the teen, she never knew.

They had just taken another load into the garage when the sound of a vehicle drew their attention. Standing in the large opening of the building with Violet and Rose, Jessa recognized Laurel's car as it appeared around the bend.

"Mama!" Rose waved at the car and started to run toward

it, but Jessa clamped a hand on her shoulder until the car had come to a stop. Once released, Rose scampered toward the driver side of the vehicle and embraced Laurel as soon as she stepped out.

Jessa and Violet followed more slowly, arriving at the car as the passenger side door opened, and Cami stepped out. She wore a sleeveless shirt and skintight jeans with heels that Jessa figured she'd break her neck in.

❦ *Chapter Seven* ❧

VIOLET hugged Cami. "Glad you could make it."

"I said I'd be here, didn't I?" Cami responded.

Jessa heard the undertone of defensiveness and wanted to make a comment on her being out of contact but held her tongue.

Violet, however, said, "Yep, but we've been trying to reach you. Laurel said you got rid of your phone?"

Cami nodded. "Was having a bit of trouble with someone harassing me. It was just easier to get rid of the phone I had there. I got a new one in Minneapolis."

The response seemed a bit odd. She could have just changed her phone number, but something had made her totally get rid of the phone altogether. That concerned Jessa, but she didn't want to press her on anything so soon after her arrival.

"Well, come on inside. We'll catch you up on what's going on," Violet looped her arm through Cami's, and they moved toward the front door. "You can get your luggage later."

"How was the trip?" Jessa asked Laurel as she and Rose joined her on the stairs. "It wasn't too much for you, was it?"

Laurel smiled. "It was wonderful. And I feel just fine. Everything is healing up just like it should. I was able to squeeze in to see my doctor this morning. She was quite surprised at what all had transpired since my last visit to her."

"I'm glad you got in to see her. Heartbeat and everything were good?"

Laurel nodded. "Everything is measuring correctly, and baby's heartbeat is strong."

They joined Violet and Cami in the kitchen. They settled down around the table to talk about what lay ahead. Rose sat by Laurel for a bit but then slipped out of the kitchen. Shortly after, Lily appeared with Rose in her wake.

Cami stood to give her a hug. "Hey, sweetie. How are you?"

"I'm great. So glad to see you again!"

Lily joined them at the table, more animated than she had been earlier in the day. Jessa worried about Cami's influence on Lily. She knew the younger girl chafed at the restrictions that had been placed on her by Gran. And since Jessa had continued with many of them, she knew Lily wasn't happy with her a good chunk of the time. She felt she could do what she wanted now that she was eighteen years old. Jessa was scared of what lay ahead for them.

"So we're emptying out all the rooms?" Cami asked, her brow furrowing. "Sounds like a lot of work."

"We've got a lot done already," Violet said. "Dean and a couple of other guys are going to come by tonight to help with the heavier pieces."

"Matt and Will are going to be here tomorrow night, so they can help on the weekend too," Laurel said.

"We're trying to get as much of the smaller pieces out so the guys can do the stuff we can't," Jessa added. "Gran's room is all done except for the bed, dressers and the sitting room furniture."

"I bet that was fun to pack up," Cami commented.

"It was interesting," Jessa replied and then turned to Laurel. "Were you able to get all the bags dropped off?"

Laurel nodded. "They were very grateful for the donations. Good quality stuff like that will definitely bring in some money for them."

"I'm glad. We have a few more boxes to donate, but I think it's stuff that's fine to go to the thrift store here in town."

After talking a bit more, Cami and Lily went to get her things from the car. Laurel gathered up a couple of boxes and some bags and took Rose to her room to begin packing it up. Violet and Jessa returned to the items from the upstairs hallway that needed to go out to the garage.

A few hours later, Dean showed up with two of his deputies who'd offered to help move the heavier furniture. He also came bearing several boxes of pizza so was warmly welcomed by more than just Violet. They got lots done, and by the time Jessa crawled into bed that night, her body was screaming for rest.

But once her body was no longer in motion, her mind kicked into high gear. Too many thoughts tumbled through her head. Cami had spent a good portion of the evening flirting with the two guys Dean had brought. Somehow Jessa had to talk to her because there was no way they could have her constantly distracting the guys working on the house. She wondered if maybe Violet or Laurel would be willing to approach her about it. Jessa was pretty sure Cami wouldn't be as receptive hearing it from her.

Though she tried not to think about it, Jessa was nervous about seeing Lance the next day. The information Gran had given her in the letter had cast parts of their past relationship in a new light, but it hadn't totally gotten rid of the anger and hurt. She just needed to keep those emotions in mind when dealing with him. Hopefully doing that would keep her from being vulnerable to him once again.

Jessa rolled to the middle of the bed and sighed. Exhaustion slowly pulled her toward sleep, but not before her thoughts touched briefly on the letter that lay in the nightstand. She would deal with that another day. *Soon.*

"Jessa? Wake up!"

Jessa turned toward the sound of her name. "Rosie? What's wrong?"

"Mama said to come get you. The guys who are going to work on the house are here."

It took a moment, but when the words registered, Jessa sat straight up in bed. "What?"

"There are two guys here. Mama said you needed to come down."

Jessa tossed back the covers and quickly got to her feet. "Tell her I'll be down in a few minutes."

Grabbing her phone from the nightstand on her way to the bathroom, Jessa checked her phone. 8:30? She'd set her alarm for 6:45. It didn't take long to realize that in her exhausted state the night before she hadn't made sure it was AM instead of PM. With a groan, she set the phone down on the vanity. Her hair had been wet when she'd gone to bed the night before, so it was all over the place, and now she didn't have time to do much of anything with it. She pulled it back in a scrunchy and quickly washed her face before applying a little bit of makeup to hide the dark circles beneath her eyes.

Thankfully she'd already laid out her clothes before she'd gone to bed the night before. After pulling on the jean capris and black T-shirt, Jessa paused, hand on the door knob, to take a deep breath and pull herself together. The last thing she wanted was to show up looking more frazzled than she already felt.

❧◦☙

"These are delicious, Laurel," Lance said as he moved the last piece of pancake on his plate to soak up the remaining syrup. "I didn't expect you to cook breakfast for us."

"Laurel lives to cook," Violet informed him as she pushed her plate toward the center of the table. "No one ever starves when she's around."

"That would be an insult to me," Laurel added.

Lance saw the little girl she'd sent after Jessa slip back into the kitchen. Laurel turned toward her.

"Jessa was still sleeping," she told Laurel.

"Really? Did you wake her up?" Laurel asked.

The little girl nodded. "She said to tell you she'd be down in a few minutes."

"Man, if I'd slept in today she would have had my butt in a sling," Cami commented dryly.

"Leave her alone," Violet warned. "She's been handling a lot the past little while. I'm not surprised it's caught up with her. She'll be beating herself up about this enough as it is, she doesn't need your help."

Cami wrinkled her nose. "Not fair, but okay. She gets a pass this one time."

Lance was a little concerned about Cami's presence. Already he'd seen how she was eyeing Josh. The last thing his cousin needed was someone like Cami. When she'd appeared in her short shorts and a tight tank top, Lance had groaned inwardly. He was going to have to talk to Jessa about it. If she gave Josh too much attention, Lance might have to reconsider having him as project manager on this job.

Laurel came around with the coffee pot and refilled their cups. She had just filled his when Jessa showed up. He wasn't surprised when his heart skipped at beat at the sight of her. She had a bit of disheveled look about her, but for someone who had just rolled out of bed, she looked pretty well put together. Her beautiful red curls were gathered into a ponytail that hung down her back. As she looked around the room, Lance noticed wariness in her blue-green gaze.

"Sorry I'm late," Jessa said as she took the cup of coffee Laurel held out to her. "It won't happen again."

"Not a problem," Lance told her. "It gave us the chance to enjoy your sister's wonderful breakfast."

"Want some?" Laurel asked her.

Jessa gave a quick shake of her head as she settled on one of the stools at the counter. She braced one bare foot on the lower rung as she crossed her legs. *Her long legs.* Cupping the mug in her hands, she raised it to take a sip.

"Have I missed anything?" she asked.

Lance shook his head. "No, we didn't talk shop. But we can now that you're here."

Jessa nodded but didn't say anything further, so Lance took that as a sign that play time was over. Standing, he picked up his dishes and put them on the counter next to where Jessa sat. As he stood near her, he got a whiff of a light floral scent that drifted on the air around her. When he turned back to the table, their gazes met and held for a brief second before she looked away.

He waited while the others cleared away their own plates. Jessa didn't say anything, but she drummed her fingers along the edge of her mug. Lance knew it was probably killing her to not be in control of this situation, but arriving late to the game meant someone else had control of the ball. And that someone was him. He was pretty sure this would be the last time she slept in during this renovation process. The thought made him grin.

He glanced her way again, grin still in place. Her brows drew together when their gazes met. Seeing the consternation on her face, he couldn't help but wink at her. One of the things he'd loved to do back when they'd been together had been to make her smile. She had been a serious one; her eyes always watching, but giving away nothing. The first time he'd made her smile, he'd lost his heart. From that point on it had been like a game for them. Him trying to make her smile, her trying not to give in. He saw snatches of that young girl in her as she regarded him seriously, her gaze once again giving away nothing.

As he'd lain in bed the night before, Lance finally accepted that seeing Jessa again had awakened something within him that he hadn't even realized had gone dormant. He knew he'd hurt her when he'd ended things between them, but he hoped she'd give him the opportunity to explain. And maybe give him a second chance. He knew they had both changed in the many intervening years, but he couldn't help but wonder if there was anything left of the spark that had once flared between them. Unfortunately, as long as Jessa viewed him as an enemy, there would be no way to find out. He could only hope that she might warm up to him as the renovations moved along.

Once everyone had settled back down in their seats, Lance cleared his throat. "I just wanted to come by this morning to run through the plans one more time. Now is the time to ask questions or bring up any concerns you might have."

"Did you plan to gut the kitchen?" Laurel asked from where she stood stacking the dirty plates.

"Yes, but I'll leave it up to you to tell me when the best time to do that would be. Obviously it would be easiest to gut everything right in the beginning. The process would move along more quickly."

Jessa glanced at Laurel and said, "We could probably make do with the kitchens in the RVs and the barbeque, couldn't we?"

Lance had a feeling his mentioning of things going faster had prompted her suggestion.

Laurel nodded. "We wouldn't have very fancy meals, but

it's doable."

"Will you be able to empty the kitchen before Monday?" Lance asked.

"We will do our best, even if we have to pay someone to come in and help," Jessa assured him.

Lance would have laughed at her eagerness to help the project along if he hadn't felt certain it was because she was trying to speed up his departure from her life. "That sounds good. I would ask that you put the fridge somewhere that it can still operate. I like to keep plenty of water on hand for my guys."

"Yep, we can do that," Laurel assured him.

"Okay, so it looks like maybe we'll need to order another dumpster to come out on Monday. If we get most the demolition done that day, it will be a good start. I don't want to get held up because we have no place to put the junk." He looked at Josh. "Can you call the dumpster company today and see if they can deliver two?"

Josh nodded. "I'll go do that now." He stood and walked out into the hall. Lance didn't miss the fact that Cami's gaze followed his cousin as he left the kitchen. Yes, he was definitely going to have that talk with Jessa.

"There will be different teams of guys coming and going over the course of the renovations. I will have some sub-contractors here working on the more specialized parts of the project. If you have a concern about any of the work or the workers, please don't go to them directly, but bring the issue to me or, if I'm not here, talk to Josh. One or both of us will be on site at all times while there is work going on."

Each of the women had a few more questions which Lance answered as best he could. Josh returned with the news that two dumpsters would be delivered early Monday morning.

"I realize this is going to be a difficult time with lots of inconveniences. I apologize for that in advance, but I hope the outcome will make it worthwhile for each of you. I know the will said something about you ladies helping out with the renovations. There are definitely things each of you could do, but likely it won't be every day. I think your grandmother was just more interested in you being all together for this process. If you want, I can let you know each day what might be available for you to do." With a glance at Cami, Lance continued, "There will be a need for proper attire when in the manor. For safety sake, we want you to be protected when working. And because this is predominantly a male environment, I'm also going to ask that there be modesty in what is worn around the guys. They don't need to be distracted while they're working. Distraction leads to accidents. We don't need any of those."

"I think he's talking to you, Cami," Violet said with a laugh.

"Shut up," Cami told her as she shot a glare in her sister's direction.

Not wanting to get into the middle of a sister quarrel, Lance quickly wrapped up the meeting. "Don't hesitate to talk to Josh or me if you have a concern. We want this to go as smoothly as possible, but no doubt there will be some bumps along the way. Just bear with us, and we'll get through it." Before anyone left the kitchen, Lance added, "Jessa, could I talk to you for a couple of minutes?"

Again her brows drew together, but she nodded. She uncrossed her legs and slid off the stool to walk in his direction.

"Can we talk in private?" Lance asked when she approached him.

She paused, looking around. "Why?"

"I just need to talk to you about something," Lance replied. "It won't take but a minute."

"Okay. Let's go to the living room."

Lance was very aware of Violet and Laurel's gazes on

them as they walked out of the kitchen. No doubt they'd have questions for their sister afterward . Too bad they'd be disappointed, because while he wanted to talk to her about their past, he knew today was neither the time nor the place for that discussion.

Jessa perched on the arm of the couch, coffee mug still in hand. "Is there a problem?"

"Not yet, but I'd like to head it off at the pass, if I can," Lance said. He put his hands on his hips, glancing in the direction of the hall to make sure they weren't being overheard. He didn't want Cami to hear them, but he also didn't want Josh to hear what he had to say to Jessa. "I need you to somehow keep Cami from zeroing in on Josh."

Jessa's eyes widened. "This is about Cami?"

Lance nodded. "I've seen her eyeing Josh since we arrived this morning. I don't want her going after him."

"Why?" Jessa asked as she lifted the mug to her lips and took another sip.

"Josh has been through a lot in his life. He doesn't need someone like Cami messing with his feelings."

"Someone like Cami?"

Lance heard the defensive tone in Jessa's voice. Initially, he was surprised given what he knew of their rocky relationship, but then he probably would have reacted the same if someone had said that about David, despite how things were between them.

"I'm sorry. I shouldn't have said it that way. Your sister is a beautiful young woman who, from what I've seen, likes to flirt. I think it's just second nature to her, I mean, she turned it on me when I first got here this morning. Until she saw Josh. From what I understand, she is only here for the month and then she's leaving. If she decides to spend that month flirting with Josh, things could get awkward."

Jessa nodded slowly. "Yes, Cami does like to flirt. But don't you think Josh could handle himself?"

"He probably could," Lance agreed. "But if you could just talk to Cami and ask her to turn her attentions elsewhere, it would help out."

"I'll do my best, but Cami isn't exactly known for listening to anything I have to say. You might have done better to talk to Violet or Laurel."

"Well, if you think she would be more receptive to them, you could maybe suggest they talk to her."

"I'll do what I can. I'm not unaware of the trouble Cami can get into." Jessa sighed. "We'll do our best to stress to her the importance of not getting in the way of the work being done here."

"I do appreciate it," Lance told her. He crossed his arms over his chest and told himself to end the conversation there, but he couldn't help himself. "So, are you and the professor an item?"

Jessa lifted a single brow. "Gareth? Not...yet. We're just friends who share some interests. We met a couple of weeks ago."

Lance was surprised she answered his question with so much detail. The "*not yet*" didn't sit well with him and yet, at the same time, it gave him hope. "He seems...interesting."

"He is," Jessa agreed without hesitation. Before he could ask anything else, she stood and said, "Was there something else? We probably need to get going on packing up more stuff."

"Nope, that was it." Lance fell into step beside her as she walked out of the living room. "Could you use a hand? Josh and I can hang around a bit to help with some of the heavier stuff."

"I don't think we're in any position to turn down help," Jessa said as they entered the now empty kitchen. "So if you have some time, there's plenty to help with. Matt will be here this evening with Will, and we have some extra help coming tomorrow as well."

Unfamiliar with the name, Lance asked, "Will?"

Jessa glanced at him. "We just found out a little while ago that our mother didn't just give birth to us girls. She apparently had a son between Cami and Lily. He's been living with a family out in California, but is on his way here today to meet us and to help out with the renovations."

"Whoa. That had to be a bit of a shock."

"Yes, it was a surprise," Jessa said. She walked around the counter to place her mug into the dishwasher. "So we'll be meeting him for the first time this evening."

"Hope it goes well." Lance remembered Violet's words about Jessa dealing with a lot. As she turned toward him, he could see the tension around her eyes and felt his heart clench. At one time, he had planned to be there for all the ups and downs in her life. The good and the bad, they were going to deal with them together. It wasn't his place to help her shoulder those burdens now, and from the looks of things, if she had her way, it never would be.

Josh came in the back door then, Cami and the others close behind him. Lance exchanged glances with Jessa, and she gave him a quick nod.

"We're going to hang around and help a bit with moving some of the furniture," Lance told Josh. "You up for that?"

"Sure thing," he said. "Happy to help wherever it's needed."

Cami smiled at him. "I love watching handsome men work up a sweat."

Josh shot Lance a look. He knew this wasn't the first time Josh had run across a woman who made her interest blatantly clear, but usually it was just in passing. The sooner someone talked to Cami, the better.

"Why don't you guys come with me, and I can show you the progress we've made already?" Jessa suggested.

In the end, it wasn't just Lance and Josh who went with Jessa. All of them tagged along as they climbed the stairs to the second floor.

"I'm focusing on my and Rose's rooms today," Laurel said as they approached the open door of what ended up being the little girl's room.

Lance was surprised to see Rose carefully folding clothes into a stack on her bed. He glanced at Laurel, who gave him a smile and whispered, "I promised her a tablet if she helped."

"Bribery is always good," Lance agreed.

"The only area that is completely done but for the larger furniture is Gran's suite," Jessa said as they moved down the hallway.

Lance noticed all the pictures that had been on the wall the last time he'd been there were gone. As he followed Jessa into the main bedroom, he saw that this was also stripped bare. "You guys have made a lot of progress."

"We weren't able to move all the heavier stuff out yet, so if you want to help with that, we'd appreciate it," Jessa told him.

"We'll certainly give it a try." Lance looked at Josh and nodded toward the chest of drawers.

"I can help with the drawers," Cami said when Josh pulled out the first one. He handed it to her without comment. After she had one in each hand, she left the room.

"I'll take a couple of those. I guess this was something we could have done earlier. I didn't even think to pull the drawers out." Jessa picked up the two drawers Josh set on the floor and headed down the hallway.

"You gonna be okay with Cami around?" Lance asked Josh. "She's definitely got her eye on you."

Josh shrugged. "I can handle her. It helps that she's not at all what I'd be looking for in a woman...if I was looking."

"Well, let me know if it gets out of hand."

With the dresser devoid of drawers, it wasn't as cumbersome to move. Together they maneuvered it out of the room and down the hall. They met Cami at the top of the stairs.

"There are still a few more drawers," Lance told her as he set down his side to adjust his grip before tackling the stairs.

When they finally reached the garage, they found Jessa waiting for them.

"You can put it over there," Jessa instructed as she pointed to an area that already held several smaller pieces of furniture.

Once it was in place, they slid the drawers back in, including the last ones that Cami brought down to them.

"Do you want us to just empty that suite of rooms?" Lance asked Jessa.

"Yes. I'm going to get to work on my room so if you need me, just yell."

Back upstairs, she disappeared into one of the open doorways and left them to tackle the remainder of the furniture with Cami. Though she seemed to behave herself, Lance was still reluctant to have her hanging around Josh much with her interest in him so blatant. He hoped Jessa was able to talk to her soon.

⁋ Chapter Eight ⁋

*J*ESSA closed the door to her room and leaned against it, letting out a long breath. This had certainly not gone as she had planned, but lately it seemed that making plans for anything was just asking for trouble. And then there was the fun conversation she'd had with Lance. She couldn't blame him for being a little wary of Cami's flirtations toward Josh. Once she had realized what was going on, Jessa would probably have said something regardless. But with Lance's request in her mind, she knew she needed to do something about it sooner rather than later.

Pushing away from the door, Jessa tried to pull together her scattered thoughts to focus on the best way to tackle packing up the room that had been hers for as long as she could remember. As she looked around, she realized that, in all likelihood, she wouldn't be returning here. Large changes loomed with larger implications for her. She was now the head of the Collingsworth family. The role her grandmother had held for most her life. And now it fell to Jessa to maintain the legacy that had been passed down.

Her gaze went to the drawer of her nightstand. Was she already continuing the legacy of secrets Gran had handed down by not revealing the contents of the envelope to Violet? She was the one who seemed most determined to find their mother. Jessa blew out a breath that lifted the hair from her forehead. If nothing else, she was beginning to understand the pressure her grandmother had operated under.

Deciding that the decision could be made later, Jessa picked up the boxes she'd brought up the night before. She pulled out a black garbage bag and opened it. Packing so that she could still find what she needed in the weeks ahead was important. To that end, winter stuff would be the first things she'd pack for storage.

She'd been working about an hour when there was a knock on the door. Pulling the scrunchy from her hair in order to fix the curls that had slipped loose, Jessa opened the door to find Lance waiting on the other side. She saw his gaze go to her hair and then to the room behind her.

"We're done with the furniture in the suite. Hope it was okay to just put it in the same area we put the dresser."

"Yes, that's perfect," Jessa said. She quickly smoothed her hair back into a ponytail; her movements deft as she wrapped the scrunchy around it again. "That was a big help. Thanks so much."

"Is there more to do? We can probably hang around for another hour or so," Lance said as he stepped back to allow her to join him in the hall.

"I guess we need the furniture out of the living room, so you can access the floors in there, right?"

Lance nodded. "It is easier when everything it out of the work area."

Jessa headed down the hallway to the stairs, very aware of his presence as he fell into step beside her. Because of her height, most men she came in contact with were either shorter than her or right at eye level with her. Lance stood a couple of inches taller than her, and Jessa had to admit she enjoyed the feeling of being smaller than him.

They found Josh downstairs in the living room, but Cami was nowhere to be seen.

"Where's Cami?" Jessa asked.

"She said something about the bathroom," Josh told her.

Jessa looked a little more closely at this man who had drawn her sister's attention. He stood about the same height as Lance and shared the same muscled figure as his cousin. No doubt that came from the work they did. Where Lance's hair was nearly black and cut short, Josh's hair was much lighter and longer in length, curling over the collar of his shirt.

"I apologize if Cami makes you uncomfortable, Josh," Jessa said.

Josh shrugged. "If I were in a different place in my life, I might be flattered." He pulled his left hand from his pocket and held it up. On his ring finger was a narrow gold band. Cami must have been slipping if she hadn't noticed that, or maybe she had and just didn't care.

Jessa glanced at Lance then back to Josh. "You're married?"

"In a matter of speaking," Josh replied. "My wife passed away a few years ago, but I am still not interested in pursuing a relationship. My ring usually works to discourage most women."

Most women didn't often include Cami. The girl had marched to the beat of her own drum since the day she, Laurel and Violet had arrived on the manor's doorstep.

"I'll make sure Cami knows that she needs to back off," Jessa assured him.

"Thanks." A smile lifted the corners of Josh's lips but disappeared quickly. Jessa realized she hadn't seen a smile from him since first meeting him earlier in the week.

She turned to Lance. "You okay to tackle this? I'm going to keep working in my room."

He nodded as he looked around. "I think we can do most of this room."

As Jessa left the living room, she spotted Cami coming down the stairs. "I think Josh and Lance have it under control in there."

Cami's eyes narrowed. "I'm sure they can always use an extra hand." She started to move past her, but Jessa grabbed her arm. Cami glared at her. "What is your problem?"

"You need to stop your flirting with Josh," Jessa told her, wishing that she'd been able to get Violet or Laurel to do this.

Cami crossed her arms and lifted her chin. "Jealous? I bet you want his attention for yourself."

A thin tendril of anger wound its way through her, but Jessa tried to hold it in check. "No, I'm not jealous. And I definitely don't want his attention. Did you not see the ring on his left hand?"

Obviously not, if Cami's reaction was anything to go by. "There's no ring on his hand."

Jessa lifted an eyebrow at her response. She saw Cami's gaze go beyond her to the entrance to the living room. She didn't intend to let Cami know Josh was actually a widower because that would totally negate the presence of the ring. "You need to back off. For his sake as well as yours. He's not available for you."

"Fine." Cami spun on her heel and stormed up the stairs.

Jessa took a deep breath and let it out.

"You handled that well."

She turned to see Lance standing in the doorway to the living room. "Thanks. I don't always do so well where Cami is concerned." Jessa glanced toward the empty staircase. "Neither did Gran, but I'm hoping I can somehow make it work. It doesn't sit well to be at odds with her."

"She's certainly different from the rest of you," Lance commented.

"Not all of us. Lily is showing some of the same rebellions Cami has. I'm hoping she isn't a bad influence on her while she's here." Jessa straightened as she realized what she was confiding in Lance. "Well, I'd better get back to work."

Lance looked like he was going to pursue the conversation but then he just nodded. "I'll let you know when we're done."

Jessa climbed the stairs, acutely aware of Lance's gaze on her. She was just glad she made it to the top of the staircase without tripping. Once in the sanctuary of her room she was able to finally relax. Hoping to create an atmosphere with a little less stress for herself, Jessa plugged her phone into the speakers and turned on her favorite playlist.

Her closet was empty of all winter clothes, only the clothing she'd still be using were left hanging. Planning to handle them last, Jessa began to tackle the boxes she'd stored mementoes and other things she'd wanted to keep over the years. The last box she found, tucked in the farthest corner of her closet, was her Lance box.

She sat down in the middle of the closet, the box on the floor in front of her. With trembling fingers, she brushed at the dust that covered the edges of it. Jessa knew she should just put it with the others, or better yet, throw it away, but instead, she lifted the lid and set it on the floor.

On the very top was the poignant reminder of the heartache she'd felt that night. The picture she'd cherished of the two of them lay ripped in two. She hadn't had many pictures of them together, because they'd rarely had someone with them to take a picture. But this was one picture Violet had taken and Jessa had taken the time to get printed.

Jessa held the torn edges of the picture together to make it one. It showed Lance smiling at the camera, his dimples in full view, as she gazed up at him. That her emotions were so visible showed the depth of what she'd felt for him. All for nothing. She lowered her hands, separating the two parts of the picture once again. After setting the picture aside, she reached for the notebook that was now at the top of the box.

She flipped through it seeing the doodles of a teenager in love. Lots of hearts and "Mrs. Evanston" scribbles on the pages along with poems and song lyrics. For someone so reserved, her emotions, tapped so deeply for the first time, had gushed out in a surprising way. Looking back, Jessa wished she'd realized then that it wasn't very often that teenage love translated into happily ever after. She traced the one recurring doodle, the one that she'd drawn of their entwined initials. After giving a copy of it to him one night, she'd told him that one day she would get it tattooed over her heart.

Ah, the foolishness of young love. Thankfully she had never taken that final permanent step. Getting rid of a tattoo would have been much harder than packing away everything in a box and shoving it into the deepest corner of her closet. And now it needed to be shoved back there. She put the notebook back in the box and replaced the lid, but for some reason, took the picture to her night stand and slid the pieces between the pages of her Bible. It was the reminder she needed of just how heartbroken she'd been back then, and she wanted it close at hand, because whether she liked it or not, Lance was as appealing to her now as he'd been back then. She put the box inside a bigger one so that she could pack things around it. The last thing she needed was for Lance to stumble across it.

Though she couldn't stop her thoughts from lingering on the box, she worked steadily until there was a knock on her door, and Laurel poked her head into the room. "We stopping for lunch?"

Jessa picked up her phone, turning off the music, and saw the time. "I guess we should."

Grateful for the break, Jessa went downstairs with Laurel. They had just reached the main floor when Lance and Josh appeared from the living room. Jessa was surprised to see Gareth following behind them.

"Hi," Jessa said as he approached her. "I didn't know you

were coming by today."

"I stopped in to see if you needed help and Lance here assured me you did."

Jessa glanced at Lance. He smiled, his dimples deepening in his cheeks. Dragging her gaze from him, she focused back on Gareth. "Have you been here long?"

"About half an hour. We've been hauling out the furniture from in there," Gareth said with a nod towards the living room.

"Well, thank you for the help." Jessa gestured to Laurel. "We're just going to get some lunch together. Would you like to stay?"

"I'd love to. Thank you."

"You two are welcome to stay as well," Jessa said as she looked once again at Lance.

"Wouldn't miss it," Lance said. "Right, Josh?"

Josh glanced at Lance and then nodded. "Sounds good."

"Just give us a couple of minutes to get some stuff together." As she turned to go to the kitchen, Jessa spotted Rose coming down the stairs. "Rosie, could you go tell Violet, Cami and Lily we'll be having lunch soon?"

She nodded and turned to head back up the stairs. Once in the kitchen they quickly pulled out a couple of loaves of bread and some deli meats. Laurel sliced up some cheese while Jessa made quick work of a few of her garden fresh tomatoes and some lettuce. By the time the rest joined them, paper plates had been set out with the food and a couple of bags of chips.

"Drinks are in the fridge," Jessa said. "Help yourself."

"Lance, did you want to say grace?" Violet asked before anyone had started to get their food.

Jessa wanted to kick herself. Seeing Gareth had distracted her. Normally she would have just said grace, but if Violet wanted Lance to do it, that was fine with her.

"Sure," Lance said with a nod. His prayer for the meal revealed an easy familiarity that told her he was most likely still involved with the faith he had held to as a teenager. Although she had wondered about the true strength of that faith when she'd found out about Daphne being pregnant. When she factored in his faith, Jessa couldn't believe he'd done what he did. But the proof had been in the pregnancy.

Faith had been important to the whole Evanston family back then, and Jessa suspected it still was. She remembered having Lance's mom as a Sunday school teacher when she had been a young teenager. Long before she had been interested in Lance, his mom had encouraged her to grow her faith and trust in God. She was probably the one woman, aside from Gran and Sylvia, who had had the biggest impact on Jessa's life.

Lance was the last one to come to the counter to get something to eat. As he built himself a sandwich, Jessa asked, "How is your mom, Lance?"

He glanced up at her. His surprise quickly slid away when he said, "She passed away three years ago."

Jessa felt the shock like a punch to the stomach. "What happened?"

"Just after Dad had accepted the job in Fargo, they found out she had cancer. It was just one more difficult thing we were dealing with back then. She fought it off and on over the next six years, but then it just became too much for her."

"I'm so sorry. I have such fond memories of your mom."

"Thanks. She was a special woman."

"How is your dad doing?" She remembered them being so close. Jessa couldn't imagine one without the other.

"It's been rough. He should be planning to retire, but he says that, without Mom, there's no reason to, so he's working as hard as ever."

Jessa glanced around and realized that while Laurel and Violet were settled at the table with Josh, there was no sign of Gareth, Cami and the two younger girls.

"They went out to the picnic table," Laurel said when Jessa looked at her.

Relieved to not have to deal with Lance and Gareth at the same time, Jessa debated where to go. Finally, she sat down next to Laurel with her plate of food.

❧ *Chapter Nine* ❧

BY the way," Lance said as he picked up his sandwich. "The other trailer is here. We pulled it into the spot behind where the first one is. I think that's what we agreed, right?"

Jessa nodded. "We're going to look like a trailer park for a while."

"You're going to need to get some cords to hook up electric and some hoses for the water," Josh pointed out.

"Maybe I'll give Matt a call and he can pick some up before he heads this way tonight," Laurel suggested.

"Probably have a better chance of getting them in Minneapolis than here," Lance agreed. "You'll want heavy duty ones."

As they finished discussing the logistics of the days ahead, the others came in the back door.

"Thought you might join us," Gareth said when Jessa met his gaze.

"Sorry." Jessa stood and took her empty plate to the

garbage can. "We were just discussing a few more things related to the renovations."

"That's okay. Your sisters kept me entertained," Gareth said with a wink.

Jessa sent Cami a sharp glance. Her sister gave her an innocent look that didn't fool Jessa for a second. And something told Jessa that Gareth was a lot more comfortable with Cami's flirtations than Josh had been. That alone didn't sit too well with how she was already feeling about Gareth.

"I didn't talk all the time," Cami said, her innocent smile sliding into a more flirtatious grin. "He's got such a sexy accent I had to let him do some of the talking."

Before anyone could add anything more to that particular conversation, Lance said, "I guess Josh and I should be heading back to Fargo. We still have a few things to finish up at the office."

"Thanks so much for lunch," Josh said as he stood.

"Are all your workers coming from Fargo?" Jessa asked.

Lance shook his head. "I was able to hire locally for quite a bit of the work."

"I think Gran would have been happy about that," Violet said. "Supporting the local community here in Collingsworth."

"Yes, that was one thing she asked of me, to do as much locally as I could. As long as I can get the quality of work I want from the locals, I'm happy to use them." Lance pointed to the back door and looked at Jessa. "Want to have a look at where we've set up the trailer? Just in case you want it moved."

Jessa followed Lance as he walked out onto the back porch and down the steps toward the trailers. He went to the one they'd just pulled out and opened the door. "Want to have a look inside? This one isn't quite as big as the other one."

Jessa climbed up into the trailer, aware of Lance's

presence behind her as she stepped into the main living area. She glanced around, surprised at how nice it was. Even though the other one had been parked for a couple days already, she hadn't even toured that one yet.

"I thought this one might work for Rose and Laurel," Lance said. "There's a master bedroom here for her and Matt, and then there's a bed at the other end for Rose."

"This would be perfect for them," Jessa agreed. "And room for Laurel to do a little cooking as well if she wants."

"Let's look at the other one," Lance suggested.

The second one was bigger, but as Jessa looked around at the sleeping spaces that Lance pointed out, she realized there was a problem. There was plenty of room for her, Cami and Violet, but now with a brother in the picture—one they didn't know—the sleeping arrangements weren't ideal.

Jessa glanced at Lance. "You said that you and Josh would also have an RV here?"

Lance nodded. "We'll be bringing mine out here when we come on Monday."

"Is it big like these ones?"

"Yes. Why?"

"Because I'm not sure any of us would be comfortable sharing close quarters with Will just yet. Given that we're meeting him for the first time tonight."

"Ah. Yes, I can see how that might be a problem." Lance smiled, his dimples making a quick appearance. "It's fine for him to bunk in my RV. There's plenty of space, and I'm pretty sure Josh will be okay with it as well."

Jessa breathed a sigh of relief. "Thank you. Now we'll just have to fight over who gets the big bed here."

"You could always rotate so you each get a crack at it," Lance suggested.

"Or just go ahead and let Cami have it and avoid any kind of conflict," Jessa said wryly.

"I wouldn't suggest doing that," Lance said, this time with a frown. "You can't give into her all the time. She's part of a family here and needs to act like it, not constantly demanding—and getting—special treatment."

Jessa glanced at Lance, trying to ignore the flutter in her stomach as she met his serious gaze. "Yes. You're right. I'm just trying to avoid conflict where I can."

"It's one thing to avoid conflict, and yet another to cater to someone as demanding as Cami."

"You sound like you have some experience with this," Jessa commented.

"David." Lance's expression darkened. "He made some bad decisions in his life and tried to take the rest of us down with his manipulations. Thankfully he's changing, but it took some tough love along the way."

Before Jessa could say anything, Lance's cell phone went. He pulled it from the holder on his belt and glanced down at the display. He stared at it for a second, then pressed a button to silence the ring and returned it to its spot on his belt.

"Thanks so much for getting these lined up for us," Jessa said, the moment to ask more about David having passed.

"Well, it will make things more smoothly having the house empty, and honestly, I think you'll find it nicer not to have to deal with the dust and everything that comes with a renovation."

"That's true. And it's probably better for Laurel to be out of that environment with her being pregnant."

Lance nodded. "I have no problem with her not working in the manor during the renovations. Your grandmother would have understood as well."

"I think maybe we'll put her on food duty. She can do lunches for the workers or something like that."

Lance smiled and once again Jessa felt that flutter in her stomach. "I'm sure the guys would love that."

"Hey, Lance." Josh poked his head into the trailer. "Daphne called. Said she couldn't get hold of you and wants to know about supper."

Lance braced his hands on his hips and sighed. "Tell her we'll be back in time."

Josh gave a quick nod and disappeared.

"Guess we'd better get on the road," Lance said. "As I've said before, just give me a call if something comes up related to the renovation over the weekend."

"I will." The flutter from earlier had gone, leaving in its place a slightly sick feeling.

Lance preceded her out of the trailer and then held his hand out to help her down the steps. Jessa hesitated before sliding her hand into his much larger one. His grip tightened as she stepped onto the metal steps and then the grass. She immediately pulled her hand from his, not wanting the flood of memories that were now lapping at the edges of her mind.

"And hey, you can call me even if it's not related to the renovation," Lance said as they walked toward the front of the house.

Jessa glanced sharply at him. He lifted an eyebrow and smiled. She had no idea how to respond, but was saved by Josh coming to meet them.

"Thanks again for lunch," Josh said, a light Southern drawl to his words.

"You're very welcome," she assured him. "Hope you don't get too tired of sandwiches. You might be eating quite a few of them in the weeks ahead."

A smiled lifted the corners of his mouth. "I'm sure they'll be just fine if today's meal was any indication."

Lance's phone rang again. He glanced at Josh before looking at the screen. Once again he ignored it, and said, "We'd better get on the road." He turned to Jessa and smiled. "See you bright and early Monday. We'll be here by eight to get things kicked off."

Jessa nodded and watched as the two men walked toward the big black truck sitting further down the driveway. Lance swung up behind the wheel while Josh climbed in the passenger side. As the truck passed in front of her, Lance lifted a hand. She returned the gesture then crossed her arms over her waist and watched as the truck disappeared from view.

"Something tells me you two have a bit more history than you let on the other day." Jessa swung around to find Gareth standing behind her. Before she could say anything, he continued, "Is it the sort of history that might preclude another bloke from having a shot at something with you?"

"We dated in high school," Jessa said, deciding that some honesty was likely the best policy here. "But it was a long time ago."

"And yet, I get the feeling that things aren't settled between the two of you," Gareth replied.

Jessa glanced back to where the truck had driven away. What could she say? Since seeing Lance that first time her emotions had been slowly unravelling where he was concerned. She'd get glimpses of the young man she'd loved, but then she had to remind herself of what had followed their break up. "Maybe not. I don't know."

Gareth sighed. "Are you in the market for another friend?"

Jessa's frowned. "A friend?"

"Well, I figure that right about now, that's all you're going to offer me." Gareth smiled. "And surprisingly enough, I'm good with that. I would still like to be able to spend time with you in your gardens."

"I'm afraid I don't know how much time I'll have for that now with the renovations starting up. But one can never have too many friends."

"On that fine note, I will take my leave," Gareth told her with a mock bow and an accent that bordered more on

British than Australian. Something told Jessa he was probably a great teacher to have, especially for a subject like English.

And once again Jessa stood and watched as he drove away. Silence settled over the manor and its surroundings. Instead of going back inside, she made her way down the path, past the RVs to her greenhouse. It was slowly dawning on her that for the foreseeable future, she was going to have very little privacy and, for someone who valued their personal space, that was going to be a big challenge. If she had just Violet and even Lily to deal with, there would be no problem, but having Cami in her space all the time would be enough to drive her round the bend.

Stepping inside the greenhouse, she paused a moment to breathe in the musky scent of earth. It only took the length of walking from the entrance to her work bench at the back for Jessa to feel some of the tension slide away. There wasn't much to do in the greenhouse now, but she spent some time cleaning up the pots and soil she would use again come fall or if she decided to plant more potted flowers at some point.

Still not ready to tackle more packing, Jessa texted Violet that she was heading into town to check in with the shop to make sure they had what they needed for the weekend. Along the way, she stopped at the land she'd bought a few years earlier for her outdoor garden.

She pulled her car to a stop at the closed gate to the property and grabbed the envelope she'd placed in her purse earlier. Leaving the car parked, Jessa pushed open the heavy gate and walked down the dirt road that ran between gardening plots and the old mobile home that sat against the tree line. She approached the wood fence encircling the garden and leaned her arms on the top. Already some plants were beginning to show above the soil, but she hoped they got a good rain soon. Six rain barrels stood along the outside of the fence and were used for watering when they had enough in them. It had been a while since they'd had a good soaking though, so they'd had to use their elevated irrigation system.

Pleased that the garden was showing progress, Jessa turned and walked to the old trailer. She knocked on the metal door and stepped back to wait for a response. Within a minute, the door opened and an older man greeted her with a smile.

"Miss Jessa! I didn't expect you by today," Rudy Jensen said. "You have a gander at the plants?"

"Everything looks wonderful, Rudy." Jessa had been a bit apprehensive when her shop manager had asked if her dad could move his trailer onto the property and care for the garden. But she'd decided to give the man a chance, and made arrangements for his run down trailer to be relocated. It had been the best decision ever as he watched over the garden without fail. He was a bit slow to move, but he never complained and seemed to take great pride in growing the plants. Last year she had tried to convince him to let her buy him a new trailer, but he'd objected vehemently. It was the only thing they'd ever really disagreed on. Jessa suspected the interior of the trailer bordered on a hoard, and that when the man eventually passed on, they'd just have to burn it. But as long as he was healthy and happy, Jessa wouldn't try to change him.

He walked with her back to the garden, his movements slow but steady. "I planted them potatoes like you told me. Still kinda skeptical 'bout it, but I guess the proof will be in the harvest."

Jessa grinned at him. "You wait. You'll see I'm right. Everything I read said you get a lot more harvest doing it this way."

Rudy shook his head. "Still not convinced."

It had taken some convincing to get him used to the raised beds planted in square foot grids, but now he was a believer. The soil above the ground warmed up much quicker than planting into soil nearer to the frost line which meant earlier planting—and harvesting—for them.

"I'm heading into the shop now," Jessa told him.

"Anything you want me to take or tell Missy?"

"Nope. She's coming by later to take me for supper. Our Friday night father-daughter date."

"Well, you two have fun." Jessa held out the envelope. At one time he'd objected, but they'd come to an agreement and he now took it without hesitation. Inside it were two gift cards and some money. One gift card was for the grocery store and the other for the gas station. She didn't want to dictate how Rudy spent his money, but always wanted to make sure he had the money to eat and be able to drive into town if he needed to.

"Thank you," Rudy said as he shoved the envelope into the pocket of his faded jeans. "Missy's birthday is this week. Gonna buy her something special."

"I'm sure she's going to be so pleased." Jessa gave the man a hug. "I'll see you later, okay? Take it easy."

"Never!" Rudy grinned at her then turned and began to amble back to the trailer.

Jessa watched for a moment, wondering how different her life might have been if she'd had a father like Rudy. He absolutely adored his daughter and had done a fine job raising her without the aid of her mother who had passed away when Missy was just a young girl. She was glad for Rudy's presence in her life. His simple approach to things was often what she needed when the urge to control everything threatened to complicate her life more than it already was.

Feeling less weighed down by all that was going on at the manor, Jessa walked back to her car and headed into town to meet up with Missy at the shop. She knew that that weight of responsibility would be back, but for now it was nice to just be able to relax a little.

ॐ

Lance watched Daphne wipe down the counters in the kitchen. She was alone. Everyone else had scattered as soon as the tense meal had ended. He would have liked to vanish as well, but he needed to talk with her.

"Hey, Lance!" Her face lit up when she spotted him walking into the kitchen.

It was stuff like that that had prompted this conversation and, hard as it was going to be, it was necessary. He leaned a hip against the island, crossing his arms over his chest. "Listen, Daphne, we need to talk."

Her movements stilled momentarily, but she quickly moved to rinse out the dishcloth and hang it over the faucet. She turned toward him, her face expressionless. "What's wrong?"

"I've been talking with Dave, and we've agreed that it's time for you guys to find your own place."

Anger flared on her face. "Why? This is a good neighborhood for the kids, and I'm able to help you with taking care of the house. I pitch in."

"I know that, and I've appreciated that, but it's no longer a healthy environment."

"What is that supposed to mean?" Daphne demanded, her brows drawn low.

"I mean, you have no claim on me, but you're acting like an over-protective mother or jealous wife."

"I should have been your wife. I was supposed to have been."

"If that marriage had taken place, it would have just made a bad situation even worse."

"If I hadn't miscarried you would have married me, but once the baby was gone, you didn't care about me anymore."

Lance didn't want to take this rocky trip down memory lane. It was a time in his life he'd tried hard to forget. "I don't want to hurt you, Daphne, but the marriage was never about how I felt about you. It was for the baby and my family. Once you were no longer pregnant, there was no reason for the marriage. You should have just moved on then."

"I loved you, Lance. Didn't you realize that?" Daphne said, her eyes dampening with tears.

❧ Chapter Ten ❧

I DON'T understand how you can say that. There was nothing between us. If Dave hadn't pulled a disappearing act before you announced you were pregnant, he would have been the one to marry you, not me." Lance told himself that enduring this again would be beneficial in the end, but he still hated doing it. "The baby was his after all."

"Then why did you agree to marry me?" Daphne demanded.

"I wanted to do the right thing for my family. We were already going through so much then, with Mom getting sick and the move." Lance sighed. "And at that point, I felt like I had nothing else to lose."

Daphne straightened, anger flashing in her eyes. "You couldn't have her, so who cared if you had to settle for me? Is this all about the calls today? The ones you wouldn't take when you were with her?"

Lance found himself a little bewildered by the venom in Daphne's tone when talking about Jessa. She didn't even say her name, but it was clear who she was referring to. "I told you this morning before we left that you didn't need to worry about supper for Josh and me. I don't know why you felt you had to call about it again. Even after Josh told you we'd be back, you still called me again."

"All I've done is try to take care of you."

"That's not your place, Daphne. It never has been." Lance had known this was going to be a hard discussion, but it was veering into the bizarre. "I'm not sure where you got the impression that it was. Dave is the one you should be taking care of. And your kids."

"Well, now you're going to just kick us out and leave us to fend for ourselves. Fine brother you are."

"Hey now," Lance said as he held up his hands. "No one said anything about kicking you out. Dave and I have talked and now that he has a good job, he's actually anxious to get into a place of your own."

"Yeah, probably some dump where the kids won't have a nice yard to play in, and I won't be able to afford to buy groceries because all the money will go to bills."

"The kids are in school now; you could get a part time job if you're that worried about money. And Dave won't make you move to a place where it's not safe for the kids."

Daphne put her fists on her hips, her grey eyes flashing. "After all I've done for you I can't believe you're going to turn your back on us this way."

"I'm turning my back on no one. Dave is in agreement about this. Do you think he doesn't see the way you treat me? It's not right. You are his wife, not mine. You should be supporting and encouraging him. He may have made some mistakes in his past, but he's trying hard to provide for you and the kids. Frankly, you don't deserve him, but for whatever reason, he loves you. So you're going to let him find you a place to live, and you're going to make it into the home that he deserves."

"It's all because you've seen her again, isn't it?"

"If you're referring to Jessa, then no, this is not about her. This is about your weird and unhealthy need to play wife to me when you already have a husband and family. It's not good for Dave or your kids, and frankly, it's making me uncomfortable in my own home." Mirroring her stance with his hands on his hips, Lance continued, "I'm going to be out of town most of the next four to six weeks. I expect you to help Dave find a place and get yourself moved into it in that time frame. I told him that I'll give you first and last month's rent to help out. I know you think I'm being mean, but honestly, I think this will be the best thing for you and Dave. It's time."

Her eyes narrowed briefly before she stormed out of the kitchen to the stairs that led to the basement where she, Dave and the kids had taken up residence almost a year ago. Lance let out a long sigh. If things hadn't gotten all weird with Daphne, he would have been perfectly fine with them staying on in the house. It was a big house with plenty of room for all of them. He and Josh had rooms on the upper floor, while his dad had one on the main floor. It was supposed to have only been for a couple of months when Dave had approached him about moving in after he lost his job. It had been fun to have the kids around. They were basically good kids, and he knew his dad loved having his only grandchildren under the same roof.

But Lance knew that Daphne's issues were getting too much when his dad had mentioned to him a few days earlier that maybe it was time for them to get their own place. That was all he needed to spur him to talk to Dave. Thankfully his brother had received it well and had agreed one hundred percent. It was probably a good thing he was going to be gone during most of the process. In fact, Monday couldn't come soon enough for him.

Jessa sat on the window seat in her room looking out over the back yard. She wished that it was already dark, but the days were lengthening until it was still light at nine-thirty. While some people were scared of the dark, it had always been a comfort for Jessa. Many times as a young girl she'd crawl back out of bed and onto the window seat after she was supposed to be asleep. She'd stare up at the stars sparkling like diamonds in the inky black sky and wonder. Were there other little girls out there like her? Ones without a mom or dad? And for the ones who had parents, what was that like? Did they get lots of hugs and kisses?

Sylvia and Jonathan had been good to her, affectionate in ways Gran had never been. But it wasn't until Violet, Laurel and Cami showed up that Jessa truly experienced a connection with someone, even though that too had been limited. She could remember the times when Laurel would come find her, and if she was sitting down, the little girl would climb up next to her and snuggle close. Violet had done it occasionally, but Cami had never really been much of a cuddler.

Tonight as she stared out toward the lake, Jessa tried to gather herself together. In a short time, she'd be meeting her brother. Though she'd tried not to dwell on it, she was angry at Gran about William. Not just that she'd kept him a secret, but that she'd decided to give him what she hadn't given the rest of them. A stable home life with people who loved and encouraged him in all areas of his life. She'd read through the information Gran had left them and had seen how he had excelled and blossomed in his life with the Millers.

While she was happy for him, she mourned what she and the others had missed out on. Sure, they had basically good lives, but at twenty-three, William seemed to have his life more together than any of them did. With the possible exception of Laurel.

A knock on the door pulled her from her dour thoughts. At her response, the door opened and Laurel poked her head into the room. "Just got a call from Matt. They're driving through town."

Jessa nodded as she stood and walked to the door.

"Ready to meet our long lost brother?"

"As ready as I'll ever be, I guess."

Walking beside Laurel down the stairs, Jessa felt the weight of responsibility more than ever since Gran had died. All of them were going to be together for the first time. She needed to make sure this went well.

They found the others in the kitchen where Violet and Rose were putting cookies on a plate while Cami and Lily sat at the table.

"So let's try and not scare him off on his first night here," Violet said as she slid the plate onto the table and smacked Cami's hand when she reached for one. "Behave."

"Yes, Mother," Cami said with a roll of her eyes.

None of them commented on the statement that was truer than most would realize. At four, Violet had been a better mother to Laurel and Cami than their own mom. It made some sense to Jessa that she'd be the one wanting to find information on the woman who had left them all. Before her thoughts could go very far in the direction of the envelope upstairs, the rumble of an engine through the open window alerted them to Matt and William's arrival.

Laurel immediately left the kitchen. Jessa and Violet weren't far behind. Cami and Lily were the last to come out onto the porch as the truck pulled to a stop. Laurel was already down the stairs and rounding the front of the truck to the driver's side when the doors opened. From the corner of her eye, Jessa saw Matt gather Laurel close, but her attention was drawn to the young man exiting the vehicle from the passenger's side.

Jessa saw right away that he had height like her and Cami, but his hair was cut short and dark brown—almost as dark as Violet's. He pushed his sunglasses to the top of his head, and she saw his eyes were a light blue.

Willing away her nerves, Jessa walked down the steps and held out her hand to him. "Hi, William. I'm Jessa."

He took her hand then grinned as he pulled her close. "Sorry, you're family, so you get a hug."

It took a second for Jessa to regain her composure at the easy familiarity with which he approached her.

"And call me Will," he continued.

"Okay, Will, this is Violet," Jessa said as she joined them. Will also hugged Violet, but unlike Jessa's surprise, Violet seemed to take it in stride.

"Nice to finally meet you, Will," Violet said with a smile.

"That's Cami and Lily." Jessa motioned for them to come closer. "Also sisters. And you might have been told that Rose was a sister as well, but she's actually Laurel's daughter."

"A niece! Cool." After hugging Cami and Lily, Will approached Rose and held out his hand. "High five?"

She grinned as she high fived him and then did a fist pump. "So do I call you Uncle Will?"

"Hey, I'm good with just plain ol' Will."

Matt and Laurel had joined them, and Matt moved his arm from Laurel's shoulders so that she could also hug Will.

"And I hear congratulations are in order," Will said as he released her.

"Thank you." Laurel laid a hand on her stomach. "We're very excited."

"Do you want to unload first or would you like some snacks that Laurel and Rosie made for us?" Jessa asked.

Will glanced at Matt. "I don't have much stuff. Should only take one load to get it all."

Matt nodded. "Me too. Even though I'm here for a week."

Laurel let out a shriek then clapped a hand over her mouth. She lowered it enough to ask, "Really?"

"Yes. I had hoped my supervisor would approve my request, but he waited until today to let me know I could have next week off," Matt said. "I figured you could probably use an extra hand for demo."

"The more the merrier," Jessa said, happy for Laurel to have her husband around a little more.

Jessa and the other sisters went back into the house, and when Matt and Will came inside, she took him upstairs to his room. "I'm afraid it's only for a couple of nights. Everything is being emptied out of the house this weekend, hopefully, so we'll be sleeping in RVs for the duration of the renovation."

"I'm not fussy about where I sleep. A sleeping bag and pillow will suit me just fine," Will assured her.

"Well, tonight you won't have to worry about that," Jessa said as she opened the door to the room she'd prepared for him. She turned on the light and stepped back to allow him into the room. "The bathroom is over there."

"This looks great." Will dumped his duffle bags onto the bed. "I'm just going to freshen up a bit and give my mom a call and then I'll be right down."

"Take your time," Jessa said. Out in the hallway she paused for a moment. *My mom.* Yet another reminder of what Gran had provided for him, but not for her and the others. Even Rose, who could have had a real mother for those first ten years of her life, had been robbed of that.

The others had gathered in the kitchen once again. Cami sat on one of the stools, her long bare legs crossed. Even with no non-related male in the immediate area, she still couldn't keep from making a display of herself. Biting her tongue to keep from saying anything, Jessa sat down next to Rose at the table.

"He seems like a real nice young man," Matt said. "I wasn't sure about driving three hours with a stranger, but honestly, it was like we'd known each other forever. I think he'll fit in well."

"Is he coming back down?" Violet asked.

Jessa nodded. "He was just going to call his mom to let

her know he'd arrived safe and sound."

"That's just all kinds of weird," Cami commented. "He's our brother, but actually has a mother."

For once, Jessa found herself agreeing with Cami, and saw Violet and Laurel nod and knew it was a unanimous observation.

"Well, at least two out of the seven us—I'm counting Rose in this—will be fortunate to have had good parents," Violet said. "By the way, I asked Sylvia Miller if she wanted to come over tomorrow to help us pack up the kitchen. I figured she'd probably want to see Will since technically she's been his grandmother all these years."

Jessa heard movement on the stairs and glanced toward the hallway in time to see Will walk in.

"Is your mom worried about you?" Jessa asked.

Will shook his head. "Not really. She knew this day was coming and has been prepared for it. I think she's relieved though, that it is happening without our grandmother present."

"Yeah. I think we're all relieved about that," Cami said with an edge to her voice.

"Pull up a chair and have some cookies," Laurel invited. "What would you like to drink?"

Will sat down next to Matt. "I'm good with whatever you've got."

Laurel laughed. "Rose is going to have milk. Cami's probably drinking water or something diet. There's juice, or we can make some coffee if you'd like."

"In that case, I think I'll go with Rose." He winked at the little girl.

"We don't know much about your family, Will," Jessa said. "Do you have siblings?"

"Yes. I have four. One is a little sister just the same age as Rose. I also have a sister who graduated this year and twin brothers who are going into grade nine."

"So your family just kind of exploded with us added in," Violet said.

"I will say I'm feeling a bit outnumbered when it comes to male siblings," Will said with a grin.

"No worries," Violet assured him. "There will be plenty of testosterone floating around in the weeks ahead."

Conversation turned to the upcoming renovations, but Jessa wasn't really in the mood. When she saw Rose stifle a yawn, she jumped at an excuse to escape.

"Laurel, can I take Rose up to bed?"

Laurel glanced at Rose and lifted her eyebrows. Rose nodded and said, "I'm tired."

It was almost an hour past her normal bedtime of eight-thirty, so it wasn't surprising, but Jessa knew she'd been anxious to meet the newest member of the family.

Rose said good night to everyone then took Jessa's hand, and they climbed the stairs together.

"Have a story to read, sweetie?" Jessa asked after the little girl had changed into her pajamas and brushed her teeth.

Rose handed her the book that was sitting on her night table and crawled under the covers. Jessa settled down on the other side of the bed, relishing the feel of the small body pressed against her arm. Though she was happy Laurel had been willing to step into the role that was rightfully hers, Jessa had struggled a lot with relinquishing the role of mother she'd had with Rose. Gran hadn't been able to really care for her as she had the older girls.

There were times Jessa had wondered if she'd ever be a mother to children of her own. It had been a small consolation to have Rose, but now that role was gone and once again she was left wondering if she'd ever be able to find that one person she could love and who would love her. The only thing that had kept her from settling for just any guy had been the knowledge of what a loveless marriage had done to her grandmother.

If Gran had said it once, she'd said it a hundred times. It was worse to be in a marriage without love than to be alone. It had become Jessa's unspoken mantra that had dictated the direction her relationships had taken over the years. She'd given plenty of guys a shot, but none of them had been able to stir in her what Lance had. Had it just been puppy love? Or had it been something that could have been lasting and strong if they'd had a chance? Although it hadn't been all that strong to begin with, Jessa reminded herself. And it was something she couldn't let herself forget.

Pulling her attention back to the familiar story she'd been reading without much thought, Jessa glanced down and saw that Rose was asleep. She slid the bookmark between the pages and placed the book on the bed beside her. Not anxious to leave, Jessa carefully reposition Rose and curled up beside her, an arm over the girl as she slept. Breathing in the gentle scent of Rose's shampoo, she closed her eyes and let out a long sigh. She knew she should get up and turn off the light and head back downstairs, but right then she was content to be in a familiar position that she had been missing.

When Jessa opened her eyes, the room was dark. She blinked a couple of times, realizing that at some point Laurel must have come in to check on them and had turned out the lights. Moving slowly, she slid out of the bed and walked through the darkness to the door. She glanced back to where Rose lay though she couldn't see anything and then let herself out into the hallway.

The house was dark and quiet as Jessa made her way to her own room. The light beside her bed glowed softly, and it didn't take Jessa long to change and crawl between the sheets. A busy weekend lay ahead so she set the alarm on her phone for seven and prayed she'd fall asleep quickly.

∝ Chapter Eleven ∾

BY Sunday night, Jessa was exhausted, and she knew she wasn't the only one. She was beyond grateful for Will, Dean and Matt's presence because they had worked hard to get the heavy stuff hauled out of the house. Sylvia had been a trooper packing up the kitchen with Laurel after she got finished loving on her grandson for a little while.

Cami had actually surprised her. Saturday morning had unfolded pretty much like she'd imagined it would with Cami complaining about everything from the dirt and dust to the broken nails she kept getting. But it seemed, by the afternoon, she'd realized no one else was putting up a fuss like she was. Not even Lily or Rose. Once she'd quit spending half her time moaning and groaning, she got quite a bit done.

Though Jessa hadn't been thrilled to have to work on Sunday, they made it to church and came right back to finish the last of the moving out. It was just past nine and things had finally settled down. Will had gone home with his grandmother since his accommodations wouldn't arrive until the next morning. Rose had bedded down without complaint in the other RV, and now Laurel and Matt were there while the four other girls were in the bigger trailer.

Once they had the water and electric hooked up, Jessa realized that they weren't really going to be roughing it in the RVs Lance had provided. The one she shared with the other three girls was quite spacious. At one end was a room with a queen bed and at the other was another room with bunk beds on each side with one even having a double bed on the bottom. In between was a kitchen, sitting and dining area. It was very lovely and made Jessa wonder if a lifestyle of RVing might not be a bad thing.

Violet had made the decision on who slept where and even though Jessa had protested, she was grateful to have been given the queen bedroom. After dealing with people—mainly Lance—all day, she knew she was going to need privacy to just unwind and regroup. She was not a huge people person to begin with, so these next few weeks were going to be a trial.

Between the kitchen in Laurel's RV and the one in theirs, they would be able to handle their meals. Both the fridge and freezer were now running in the garage, but they were going to have to make trips into town for their laundry. Laurel had already stepped up to say that she'd be happy to take care of the "household chores" such as cooking, cleaning and laundry since working with the dust and chemicals in the manor weren't the best idea given her condition. Rose would be her helper since it wasn't an ideal environment for her to be in either.

Jessa flopped down on her back on the bed and stared up at the ceiling fan that was lazily circling. Thankfully they were running the air conditioners in both units, so the room wasn't too warm.

"Jess?"

She pushed herself into a sitting position to see Violet in the doorway. "What's up?"

"We're all wanting to take showers. How about you?"

"Yeah. I feel awful grungy."

"I think we can still pop into the house to use the showers

there. Matt is going to talk to Lance and Josh tomorrow about doing something with the RV's and the septic tank for the house. That way we don't have to worry about constantly emptying the tanks here."

There were so many little details that Jessa hadn't thought about. Usually she liked to make sure all the things like that were taken care of, but in this case she just had no idea. Thankfully Matt had experience that was coming in handy, and she had no doubt that, between him and the other two guys, they'd figure something out.

After Violet had left, Jessa gathered up a towel, some clean clothes and her toiletries. Back at the house she went ahead and used her own bathroom, feeling much better when she got back to the RV freshly showered. Everyone seemed ready to call it an early night, and before it was fully dark outside, all four of them in the RV had settled into their temporary beds.

♾

Lance let out a long breath when he finally turned his truck onto the highway and headed for Collingsworth. It had been a super early morning for them because he wanted to be there before eight. Thankfully it had just been a matter of getting up and heading out since they'd hooked up and packed the fifth wheel the night before. Josh followed behind him in his truck so that he'd still have wheels if Lance had to leave the worksite for any length of time.

Usually a job of this size would be stressing him out, but right then, he felt as if he was leaving the biggest stress behind in Fargo. He'd felt bad about his dad having to deal with it all, but the older man assured Lance that it wasn't a problem. In fact, his dad had felt it would be better if he wasn't around. The weekend had been anything but heavenly around the house. Daphne had made sure that each and every person in the house knew how very unhappy she was about the impending move. Never had Lance been so glad to leave his own home.

Now on the road headed east with the sun just beginning to peek above the horizon, Lance could finally relax. He pressed a couple of buttons and soon his favorite Christian music filled the cab of the truck.

He didn't think for a minute that the weeks ahead would be without problems, but he found himself very excited about the project. Not only was it a huge job with a great paycheck, but he was going to be working alongside Jessa. He could tell it wasn't exactly something she was thrilled about, but he was hoping that they could get to know each other again and maybe discover the spark from years ago was still there. God knew no other woman had managed to engage him like Jessa had in the years since they'd been forced apart. Oh, he'd tried. After all, he'd figured that there was no chance for him with Jessa, so he'd tried to move on. He'd had a couple of longer relationships but in the end, both women had ended it with him stating they didn't feel his heart was fully in the relationship.

He hoped that this time with Jessa would accomplish one of two things. Either they'd rediscover the spark and give their relationship another try, or he'd realize that there was nothing left there and it would finally free him to move on. Since ending the relationship had not been what either of them had wanted, it stood to reason that a part of him still wondered if there was a chance. Discovering Jessa wanted nothing to do with him or that there was nothing to resurrect might help him to put their relationship well and truly in the past.

Though he would have liked to drive faster, pulling the fifth wheel dictated a slower pace. Thankfully there were no issues, so they pulled up to the manor a little after seven. He waited while Josh parked his truck off to the side and then made his way on foot to help direct Lance into position. It wasn't difficult to back his fifth wheel into place because he was used to doing it.

Since they'd done this many times before, it didn't take long to get the trailer level and stabilized enough to unhitch it from the truck. While Lance completed the set-up, Josh got behind the wheel and parked the truck where he'd parked his. He had just finished getting the slide-outs into position when a man climbed out of the middle trailer and headed his way.

The tall man held out his hand as he neared. "You must be Lance. I'm Matt Davis, Laurel's husband."

Lance gave Matt's hand a firm shake as he observed the brown haired man with some curiosity. Here was someone who had managed to not only love, but keep, one of the Collingsworth sisters. He wondered if Matt might give him some pointers. "Nice to meet you. I wasn't sure you'd be around for much of this. Laurel said she didn't think you could get time off."

"Yeah. I just found out Friday that my supervisor had approved my request. I'll be here for the week." Matt glanced at the trailer. "Nice outfit you've got."

"Yep. Lots of lakes around to go fishing, so I bought this a few years back," Lance said as he patted the side of the trailer. "It's definitely coming in handy for this job."

"Thanks for getting those other two as well. They're just perfect for what we need. And surprisingly comfortable. Wasn't sure with my height that I'd be sleeping too well, but no problems last night."

Lance heard footsteps and turned to see Josh approaching. His cousin tossed him the keys to the truck as Lance introduced him to Matt.

"Listen, I was wondering about a possible alternative for the plumbing situation for these three trailers," Matt said after shaking Josh's hand.

They spent the next several minutes tossing around a few ideas and between the three of them, they came up with what Lance thought would be the best solution. "I'll have a couple of my guys get to work on it right away."

"Morning."

Lance swung around and smiled at Jessa. "Good

morning. Ready to get this underway?"

"More than ready," Jessa said. "Are the dumpsters due soon?"

Lance was kind of disappointed that she was all business this morning, but wasn't too surprised. She wore a pair of loose fitting faded jeans and a long sleeved shirt though the sleeves were pushed up to her elbows. He saw that she'd taken his advice and gotten herself a pair of heavy work boots. Her beautiful red hair was pulled back tight in a braid, out of the way for the hard work to come.

And Violet looked similar when she showed up. She held a travel mug in her hand and took a sip from it as she joined them. "Morning, guys."

Before any further discussion could get underway, noise from the road drew Lance's attention. Shoving his hands into the pockets of his jeans, he headed toward the front of the house, Josh beside him. With the arrival of the dumpsters, the pieces were falling into place for the start of the job ahead. All that was left was for his guys to show up, and they'd be ready to go.

♀∘♂

The muscles that hadn't been screaming the night before were certainly making their presence known as the day progressed. Jessa hadn't thought of herself as out of shape, but clearly her body wasn't made for work like this. Everything ached, and she was regretting that she didn't having a nice deep tub to soak in at the end of the day.

The good part was that everyone had worked hard. Even Lily and Cami had done more than Jessa had imagined. Their help the day before moving furniture hadn't just been a fluke. And Lance may have been the boss, but he pitched in as much as his guys had. Josh, Matt, and Will had also worked up quite a sweat over the course of the day. Jessa understood now why Lance insisted his guys have access to plenty of water. It would be easy to get dehydrated sweating so much in the heat of the day. They'd stopped for a quick lunch, but then had gone back at it.

"Okay, guys, round up!" Lance shouted. Guys that had been in various places in the house began to join them in what was left of the living room.

Jessa stood to the side with Will, Violet and the other girls. Matt and Josh stood with Lance as they waited for the guys to gather.

"Thanks, everyone, for your hard work today," Lance began. "We got a ton done. They'll be coming to get the bins shortly. I am having them drop off another one because we still have more stuff that needs to go and these two are full. We'll finish off the little that's left of the demoing tomorrow and then move on to rebuilding this place."

Jessa stood trying to focus on Lance's words, but she found her thoughts kept drifting. She'd seen glimpses of leadership in Lance as a teen when he'd been on the football team and in the youth at church, but never had she imagined him in the position of owning his own company. But he was more than just an owner; she had seen that as well. He wasn't afraid to work alongside his employees, and he took care of them too. Frequent breaks, constant supply of cold water and he'd given Laurel money to buy food for their lunches.

Jessa just hoped the rest of the days went as well as this one had, even though she knew that was unlikely. It was just after five when Lance called it a day for the guys. They'd probably work longer days in the future as needed, but Jessa was glad the first day was over.

Once Lance dismissed the guys, and they began to leave, Jessa headed for the trailer. A blast of cool air greeted her as she opened the door. Enjoying the blessed coolness, she made her way to her room and flopped on her back on the bed. She heard the others come in as well, each talking about how tired they were.

"Hey, Jess?"

Jessa lifted her head to see Laurel standing in the

doorway. "What's up?"

"Do you want to try and eat supper together in one of the trailers or should we eat wherever?"

She propped herself up on her elbows, wincing at the strain on her upper arms. "I don't think any place is big enough for us all to sit down. If we want to have meals like that, we're gonna need to get some more patio furniture. For tonight, just have people dish up where you cooked the food and let them sit wherever."

"Okay, sounds good. Supper will be ready around six. I think some wanted to get cleaned up before eating." Laurel disappeared, closing the sliding door behind her.

Jessa turned and crawled to the pillows and flopped down. *Just five minutes.* Just a quick break before getting ready for supper.

"Where's Jessa?" Laurel asked.

Lance glanced around at the people gathered outside the trailer, noting her absence.

"She's sleeping," Violet volunteered. "I peeked in on her, and she was passed out on her bed. Just save her some food for when she wakes up."

Lance wasn't surprised that she'd conked out. The woman had worked as hard as any of the men during the demo.

"Dean, do you want to pray?" Laurel asked of the man who had arrived just a few minutes earlier and had been introduced as Violet's boyfriend. He'd had a small girl in tow who was now holding hands with Violet.

Once the prayer had been said, they filed in to fill paper plates with the food Laurel had prepared. Lance was glad to see there was plenty because he knew he was hungry, and he was pretty sure he wasn't the only one.

The loaded plates of Josh and Matt when they joined him at the picnic table they'd set up under the awning of his trailer backed up that assumption.

"Your wife is quite the cook," Lance commented to Matt after he'd polished off his first piece of chicken.

"Yes. That she is," Matt agreed with a grin. "It's a good thing I have such a physical job or I'd probably be twice this size with the way she cooks."

"I guess this is where the men are hanging out," Dean said as he set his plate on the table and settled down on the bench next to Matt. Will was right behind him with his plate loaded with food.

The sound of an approaching car engine had them turning toward the front of the house. Before anyone could appear there, Lily walked past them.

"She's got a date."

Lance glanced over to see that Violet had joined them. She had a plate in one hand and a folding chair in the other.

Dean got up to open it for her. "Did you want a drink, babe?"

"I think I left it inside the trailer," Violet said.

"I'll get it for you."

When Dean returned, he had the other women in tow with a couple more folded chairs. Apparently the two younger girls had opted to stay inside the trailer, and there was still no sign of Jessa. It was interesting, however, to watch the interaction between the women and their significant others. And as he'd wondered about Matt with Laurel earlier, Lance was also curious about Dean and Violet. Though Cami wasn't directing her flirting to Josh, she hadn't completely shut down the suggestive remarks and body language. He wondered what Will thought of his sister.

"There's nothing fancy for dessert," Laurel told them as they finished their meal. "But there are some cookies and ice cream if you want."

The meal wound down, and everyone pitched to help

clean up. Though it wasn't the most environmentally friendly approach, they had pretty much gone 100% disposable because of the hassle of trying to wash everything in the small sinks in the trailers.

"I'm gonna go do a walk through at the house," Lance said to Josh. "Want to come with?"

Josh didn't hesitate to join him. No doubt eager to be away from Cami.

"Mind if I tag along?" Dean asked. "It would be interesting to see this old place stripped down to the studs."

"Sure, the more the merrier," Lance said with a wave of his hand.

In the end, it was just Dean and Will who joined them. The manor seemed much larger and less intimidating without all the walls and furniture in place. He knew that Julia Collingsworth wasn't paying attention to what was going on down on earth, but Lance hoped that if she had, she would be pleased with the direction things were moving in.

One thing that did puzzle him and was something he had been putting off, having not even mentioned it to the Collingsworth ladies, was Julia's insistence that he break ground for a gazebo in the lightly forested area south of the large back yard. When he'd questioned her about it, she'd said that she'd always wanted a structure there to enjoy the beautiful surroundings. She'd been very specific about the location, and Lance knew he needed to go out and have a look at it in the next day or two.

It was something that could wait until the end of the renovations, but he was thinking it might be a better project for the ladies to work on. The work that was to start inside the manor was more skilled labor, and they would probably just slow the workers down. He could spare a couple of guys to work the pagoda or even have Will help him show the women what to do there. And at some point, he was going to have to convince Jessa to take a trip to Fargo with him to pick out cabinetry, countertops, tiling and appliances. That would also have to happen sooner rather than later. They could get the stuff locally, but he had people in Fargo he liked to deal with directly who gave him good deals on their product.

Convincing her to go with him would probably be one of the biggest challenges of this whole job.

❧ Chapter Twelve ❧

JESSA rolled over and groaned in pain. She kept her eyes closed as she groped around the bed beside her for her phone. Finding it, she lifted it to her face and cracked an eye to look at the time. Both eyes popped opened when she realized she'd slept a good chunk longer than the five minutes she'd planned on. Her stomach growled as if just realizing it had missed supper.

Moving slowly, she swung her feet over the bed to the narrow space between the edge of the bed and the wall. She pulled the elastic from her braid and loosened it, allowing her curls to spring free from the confinement. Before she faced anyone though, she was going to take a shower. The dirt and grime from the day felt heavy on her skin.

She grabbed her towel and shower stuff and slid the door open to the rest of the trailer. Thankfully, it was empty, so she didn't have to talk with anyone. She just needed a few more minutes to herself to wake up.

Feeling one hundred percent better after her shower, Jessa stepped out of the trailer. She spotted her sisters at a picnic table. Addy and Rose were sitting there as well with coloring books and crayons in front of them.

Laurel spotted her right away and stood up. "Hey, sleepyhead! Want some supper?"

"There's food left?" Jessa asked. "I figured the men would have inhaled your delicious cooking."

"Not to worry. I made sure to save you some before they got a crack at it."

Jessa followed her into the trailer.

"Do you want me to heat it up for you?" Laurel asked as she uncovered a plate with fried chicken and potato salad on it. "I can put the chicken on a separate plate."

"I think it will be fine this way," Jessa said, eager to get something into her rumbling stomach. She took the plate from Laurel.

"Just water to drink?" Laurel asked as she opened the small fridge.

Jessa nodded. "Thanks. You're spoiling me. If we'd slept through dinner with Gran, we'd be going hungry."

"It's a personal affront if someone in my vicinity goes hungry." Laurel smiled. "To be honest, I'm in my element cooking for this crowd."

Jessa shuddered. "Better you than me. Just make sure you don't overdo it."

"I'm fine. Rose has turned into a great helper for me." Laurel led the way out of the trailer. "I get plenty of time to rest. The challenge is coming up with new meals for each day."

As they approached the picnic table, Jessa saw that the men had returned from wherever they had been. Lance was pulling some more folding chairs out from the storage section of his trailer. As she sat down next to Rose, he glanced over, saw her and smiled.

After he had set up the chairs, he settled on the bench across the picnic table from her. "Guess we wore you out today, huh?"

Jessa pulled apart the bun Laurel had added to her plate and spread some butter on it. "Yeah, I only planned to lie down for five minutes. Next thing I know, almost two hours had passed."

"Well, hopefully tomorrow will not be as heavy a day for you guys."

"We made a lot of progress today, didn't we?" Jessa commented. She was a bit self-conscious eating in front of him, but her growling stomach was going to be more embarrassing if she didn't get something in it, so she took a bite of the potato salad.

"Yes. It went very well for the first day," Lance agreed. "I would say we'll be done with the demoing by noon tomorrow. After that, the work shouldn't be as demanding for you ladies."

"I'm glad to hear that," Cami piped up from where she sat. "I thought I was in pretty good shape, but today was crazy."

"Well, from here on out, my guys will be doing most of the heavy work." Lance looked at Jessa. "What I need from you is a day when you'd be willing to go with me to Fargo."

Jessa almost choked on the piece of chicken she was chewing. "Why?"

"We need to pick out stuff for the kitchen and the bathrooms. And look at flooring too."

The thought of spending a whole day alone with Lance made her stomach clench. "There's nothing local?"

"There is, but the people I usually deal with in Fargo have a better selection and will give me a better deal."

"When do you need to do this?"

"The sooner, the better. Some of it will be custom and take a few weeks to arrive. Ordering it now will allow for delays and possible issues along the way."

Jessa saw the logic in what he was saying, but really didn't want to be alone with him for that long. She wondered if she could talk Violet or even Cami into coming with them. For now, she just nodded. She'd try to bribe her sisters later behind closed doors.

The rumbling in her stomach was replaced by a flutter of nerves, but Jessa forced herself to continue eating. She just had to keep it professional. Lance may think what happened all those years ago was irrelevant, but to her it wasn't. He probably didn't even know that she was aware of all that had transpired after they'd broken up, and he'd moved to Fargo. It was hard to look at him and not see the young man she'd loved. Thankfully not far behind that was the remembrance that he was also the young man who'd cheated on her.

Her throat tightened, and it took effort to swallow the bite of potato salad she'd taken. She lifted the glass of water Laurel had given her and took a sip. Talk continued around her, and thankfully Lance was now engaged in conversation with Dean. After eating most of what was on her plate, Jessa took it back into the trailer. She cleaned up the plate and silverware and refilled her glass. Not in any rush to return to the group outside, she sank down on the couch in Laurel's trailer. Part of her wished she'd just slept right on through until morning. Dealing with Lance was resurrecting too many things she'd thought were long buried.

She stared at the glass in her hand, swirling the water as she thought about the weeks that lay ahead. If Lance would just keep his distance, it wouldn't be so bad, but no matter which way she turned, he was there. And given that she was the one he'd come to with any questions regarding the project since Gran was gone, there was just no way to avoid it.

The latch clicked on the door of the trailer and Jessa looked up to see Laurel step inside.

"You okay?" she asked as she came and sank down on the couch next to Jessa.

"I'm fine." Jessa gave her a smile. "Just find it a little

stressful to deal with Lance."

"Wish I knew what Gran was thinking when she hired him," Laurel said, lacing her fingers across the small bump of her stomach.

"She was trying to make amends," Jessa told her. Mentioning that brought back to mind the letter that was now packed in her bag in the other trailer.

"How do you know?"

Jessa realized she'd back herself into a corner of sorts, but it had to come out eventually. "I found another letter from Gran when I was cleaning out her room."

Laurel straightened, surprise in her eyes. "Really? Why didn't you say anything sooner?"

"I wasn't sure what to do." Jessa looked back down at the glass she held in her hand. "The letter to me explained about Lance."

"What was there to explain?" Laurel asked. "I thought she didn't like Lance, so didn't want you together."

"Actually, that's just what I told you at the time. What really happened was that Lance broke up with me. But my little lie was apparently more truth than I'd realized. Gran did force Lance to break up with me. It wasn't that Gran didn't like Lance; it was that she had information that made her think a relationship between us would be wrong." Jessa took a breath and slowly let it out. "Elizabeth had told her that my father was Lance's uncle."

"Whoa." Laurel's eyes widened with surprise. "I guess I can see how that would be a problem."

Jessa nodded. "Obviously if we were cousins, it wasn't a good thing. Gran confronted the man and he denied it, but of course he would. Agreeing would have meant he had had sex with an underage girl. I think Mama told Gran it was him just to upset her. Gran didn't realize until recently that Mama had actually told me my father was someone else. I never spoke to Gran about her. Any time I had tried to when

I was much younger, she always got upset. So when she realized that perhaps she'd made a mistake, she tracked down Lance's uncle again, and this time asked for a DNA test. He agreed, and the results came back that he wasn't my father."

"So there was no reason for her to have broken the two of you up?" Laurel asked.

"Nope. No reason." Jessa took a sip of her water. "But in the end it was for the best."

"What do you mean?"

Before Jessa could answer, Rose poked her head in the door. "Jessa, Maura's here."

"Really?" Jessa was excited to see one of her best friends. Maura had taken off on a month long trip to Europe with her mom as soon as school had ended. Jessa left the trailer with Laurel following behind her.

She was surprised to see Lance standing, arms crossed, talking to Maura apart from the group. Maura placed her hands on her hips and gave an emphatic shake of her head.

"Hey, Maura," Jessa said as she approached them, wondering how well they knew each other.

Both Maura and Lance turned toward her, stormy expressions on their faces. Before Jessa could comment, Maura hugged her and then linked her arm through Jessa's and moved them away from Lance and the group.

"It's so good to see you," she said as she walked them toward the back of the manor. "I thought I'd stop by and see how things were going on the renovations."

"It's good to see you too, but what's going on with you and Lance? Do you guys know each other?" Jessa allowed her to lead the way to the swing on the back porch. "You two didn't look very happy with each other."

"It was a long time ago," Maura said as she set the swing in motion.

"Sure doesn't seem like it," Jessa countered. "You two looked like you were arguing."

Maura sighed. "We had an...encounter in high school that left us with a not so great opinion of each other. I was just surprised to run into him here." She glanced over to Jessa. "What is he doing here?"

"Gran hired him to do the renovations."

"Seriously? I thought she hated him."

Jessa told her what she'd shared with Laurel earlier. "So he showed up a couple of weeks ago and yeah, it's been a boatload of fun."

"Well, just watch yourself. It's not like you guys can pick up where you left off," Maura said. "You have both changed a lot in the years since you were last together."

"Yes, I know." Jessa stared out at the trees. Dusk was slowly pushing the sun from the sky. It was the part of the day she enjoyed the most, but right now, she felt more like a mass of raw nerves. "I just want to fast forward through these next few weeks, and then move on with life." They sat in silence for a couple of minutes and then Jessa asked, "How was your trip?"

Though Jessa was very much a homebody, she enjoyed hearing about Maura's trips. She usually took at least one cruise a year with her mom, sometimes more. She'd been married for a couple of years, but the guy had dumped her and ever since then, she had focused on just enjoying life and collecting experiences and memories.

"One of these days I'm going to take you with me," Maura told her with a smile. "Just once before you die you need to leave this continent."

Jessa just shrugged. They'd had this discussion before. Unlike Violet, she'd never had the urge to travel. Not that she ignored what went on in the rest of the world. Jessa made sure to stay informed about things that were occurring around the globe; she just had no real interest in travelling to see those places.

"I'd better head for home. I just wanted to come see you and how the renovations were going."

"Want to have a look? The place looks bare and kinda sad." Jessa stood and walked to the back door. Maura followed behind her as they stepped inside. With the sun setting, the interior was dark, so Jessa flipped the switch near the back door to shed some light in the kitchen area. "Watch your step. There's still some stuff laying around."

"Wow! This place really is gutted," Maura commented. "I bet it's going to look beautiful when it's all done."

"I hope so, because it wouldn't have been worth the inconvenience if it isn't."

They wandered through the lower floor and then went upstairs. There were no walls remaining on the second floor, just the framework. Jessa tried to explain what she remembered of the floor plans as they walked around.

"So you're going to have a whole suite to yourself?" Maura asked.

"I would like to if I'm going to go with the bed and breakfast idea."

"I think it would be good for you. Something new and fresh to focus on." Maura grinned. "If you're not going to leave the state, at least mixing it up would be a good thing. Meet any interesting guys while I was gone?"

"Actually," Jessa began as they walked back toward the staircase. "I went out for dinner with a professor from the college. He is into gardening like me."

Maura shot her a surprised look. "Do tell!"

Since not much had happened yet, by the time they got to the back door after shutting off the lights, she'd basically told Maura everything.

"So no spark?"

"No. Nothing beyond an intellectual connection over the

gardening." Night had settled more deeply over the manor while they'd been inside, so Jessa moved carefully down the back stairs.

"That's a start, isn't it?" Maura once again linked her arm through Jessa's.

"I thought it might be, but it turns out it isn't." They rounded the corner of the house and Jessa saw that little white twinkling lights cast a soft glow on the group still seated around the picnic table.

Maura tugged her arm in the direction of the front of the house. "I think it would be best if I just headed for home."

Puzzled anew by Maura's reaction to Lance's presence, Jessa didn't resist and walked with her along the side of the house to the driveway. "I'm glad you came by. I was wondering when you were going to get back."

"If you need a decent shower or a tub to soak in, feel free to come by my place," Maura said as she gave her a quick hug.

Jessa laughed. "I just might take you up on that. This work is really kicking my behind. I'm more out of shape than I realized."

As she watched Maura drive away, Jessa wished she could have gone with her. She didn't fancy returning to the group gathered outside the trailers. She could handle working alongside Lance, but add socializing on top of that, and it was more than she wanted to deal with.

"I didn't know you were friends with Maura."

❧ *Chapter Thirteen* ❧

JESSA spun around at the sound of Lance's voice. She couldn't see him very well in the dark, so there was no way to read his expression. "Yes, we became friends when we worked together one summer at her parents' florist shop. I know she was a year or so older than me, but why are you surprised we are friends?"

"Because last I heard from her was that she didn't like you. In fact, she said something along the lines of you being a spoiled Collingsworth brat."

Jessa jerked back at the words. "What? Why would she say something like that?"

"Because when she tried to flirt with me, I told her I was already taken. By you."

Jessa closed her eyes briefly. Butterflies warred with a sick feeling in her stomach. Not once had Maura said anything, even when Jessa had confided in her about the break up. And it had been Maura who had told her about Daphne being pregnant, and them getting engaged. She didn't know what to think about the person whom she had thought was her best friend for the past decade. But it certainly explained Maura's reaction to Lance's presence.

She felt movement and suddenly Lance was close, his hand on her arm. The scent of his cologne swirled around her and her already on edge emotions tangled more.

"Listen, I didn't mean to upset you. I was just really shocked to see her show up here and then to hear you say she was your best friend."

Pressing a hand to her stomach, Jessa said, "She never told me anything about liking you back then."

"Maybe I'm out of line saying anything," Lance said, his voice low in the darkness. "It was a long time ago. It seems like she moved past it quickly enough to become friends with you."

Jessa hoped that was the case. But she couldn't help but wonder if she should talk to Maura about it. Was it best to just leave the past in the past? She did remember, thinking back, how she thought it was strange how spiteful Maura had seemed toward Lance when she'd told her about the Daphne situation. At the time, she'd eventually just dismissed it as Maura being upset on her behalf after having to break up with him. But now...

"Yeah, it's all in the past," Jessa said, surprised at how steady her voice sounded. "We were different people back then."

"Yes, we were," Lance agreed. "But I'd like to get to know the person you are now."

"I'm sure that's inevitable, given our close working and living situations," Jessa said, trying to keep her tone light. She stepped away from him and ignored the bereft feeling at the loss of his closeness. If he thought she was going to be the pushover she'd been as a teenager, he had another thing coming. He'd been able to blind her to the fact that he was cheating back then, but now she wasn't going to be put in that position ever again with him. "I know we've got another busy day tomorrow, so I think I'm going to head for bed. See you in the morning."

Without waiting for him to respond, Jessa turned and headed toward the trailer farthest from Lance's. She called out a good night to the remainder of the group and opened the door to climb the narrow steps into the trailer. Thankfully it was empty, so she quickly went through her night time routine before sliding between the sheets of the bed. She picked up her Bible from the nightstand and took out the ripped picture. She stared at it, willing herself to remember the heartache. After sliding it back with the Bible's pages, she spent some time doing her reading for the day and praying. She wanted to pray about the situation with Lance, but didn't know what exactly to pray for. In the end, she just asked for the ability to deal with him professionally and put the hurt aside.

Even though she had slept earlier, as soon as she slid down onto the pillows, heaviness tugged at her eyelids again. She welcomed sleep because she didn't want to think anymore. Didn't want to think about Lance and the stuff he'd told her about Maura. Or the information Gran had left her and the letter that still lay unopened in her purse.

Sleep was the best way to get a break from all of it.

Lance returned to his chair outside the trailer. Will and the other women sat at the picnic table chatting, but Lance only listened half-heartedly to their conversation. Josh sat next to him, his legs stretched out, but he appeared to be paying more attention to the others. Lance knew he was to blame for Jessa's distance with him. After all, he'd broken things off with her. All he wanted was to have the opportunity to apologize and explain.

He was unattached. She appeared to be unattached. He just couldn't believe she didn't harbor the same curiosity to see if what they once had was still there. Of course, now he knew Maura was in the picture, which cast things in a slightly different light. An awful feeling crept over him as he turned his gaze to the trailer, watching as the light in the rear of the RV winked out. He knew Maura and Daphne had been friends. Was it possible Maura had shared what had transpired between him and Daphne after the move to Fargo?

If that were the case, it would explain an awful lot about how Jessa was acting toward him. He didn't want to dredge up that part of the past, but if she did know about the engagement, he somehow needed to clarify what had happened. Maybe that would be a good topic for the three hours he'd have her undivided attention on the way into Fargo. Certainly the manor, with so many people around, was not the place.

"Well, guys, I'm going to call it a day," Laurel said. She stood and pressed a hand to her back. "Sorry, I'm not up to doing breakfast as well, but I've put food in each of the trailers' fridges so you won't go hungry."

"No worries," Lance assured her. "We appreciate all you're doing for us in the food department. I might actually gain weight while on the job the time around."

He stood, and Josh followed suit. It didn't take long to put up all the chairs in case of rain and then he climbed into his trailer. Will had dropped his bags off earlier that morning, and now Lance showed him where he could put his stuff and sleep.

After a quick shower, he climbed into bed and called his dad to see how the day had gone there. He wasn't surprised to hear Daphne was still on the war path, but thankfully his dad was taking it all in stride. Though there was plenty to keep him awake, he'd long ago developed the ability to shut down his mind and just rest when he had the chance. Another busy day lay ahead, and he needed to be at the top of his game.

৵৽৵

Having been tired enough to fall asleep quickly, Jessa had hoped she would stay asleep, but that hadn't been the case. When her alarm went the next morning, she dragged herself from the bed, not at all looking forward to the day.

Thankfully the morning went as smoothly as the previous day had. By noon, Lance let them know that the demo part was pretty much done. The guys were moving onto the rebuilding part of the process after their lunch break, and Lance told the women they didn't have to be part of that. Jessa wasn't sure what he planned to have them do, but she had some other things to take care of.

After a quick lunch and freshening up, Jessa headed to her greenhouse for a bit and then to the garden plots to see Rudy. After making sure everything was okay with him and the garden, she went into the shop to check in with Missy.

Being around the things and people she loved helped to ease the tension she'd felt lately. Normally one of those people would be Maura, but Jessa knew seeing her friend wouldn't relieve any tension. Particularly given what she now knew. She didn't want to bring up the past, but it was unsettling to think that someone she had trusted for this long had thought so badly of her.

"I'll come by again later in the week," Jessa said once she and Missy had finished going over the shop business. "But give me a call if anything comes up. Thanks for picking up my slack these days."

"Not too much slack to pick up. You've always had this place running like a well-oiled machine." Missy gave her a hug. "Just enjoy the time with your family."

As Jessa stepped out into the warm afternoon sun, she wanted to laugh. While it hadn't gone as badly as it could have, there hadn't been much family bonding so far. Of course, the month was young. There was plenty of time left for it to get better. Or worse.

When she pulled to the curb in front of Maura's house, Jessa wasn't given the opportunity to change her mind as her friend was out in the front yard and spotted her right away. She waved, and then pulled off her gardening gloves as she walked toward Jessa's car. Taking a deep breath, Jessa pushed open the door and stepped out.

Maura shaded her eyes with a hand. "I didn't expect to see you today. Need a soak in the tub?"

Jessa shook her head. "Just wanted to talk."

Her friend slowly lowered her hand and nodded. "C'mon in. I could use a break anyway."

Jessa followed Maura into the house and settled on a stool at the counter in her kitchen.

"Want a drink?" Maura asked as she pulled a couple of glasses from the cupboard.

"Just water," Jessa said, wondering if she could just pull this off as a casual visit and not delve into what Lance had revealed the night before.

Maura filled both glasses from her water dispenser and set one on the counter in front of Jessa. She stood on the other side of the counter, head tilted to the side. A striking woman with grey eyes that contrasted against her light brown skin, Maura usually had a ready smile, but today her expression was resigned. "I guess you and Lance talked after I left."

"Yes. And I'm confused." Jess traced a finger through the moisture on the outside of the cold glass. "Was he telling the truth?"

"Did he tell you that I liked him and despised you?"

Jessa nodded. "Something along those lines."

"He was telling the truth." Maura sighed. "I was a mess back then. Trying to find my identity. Watching my parents struggle to get their business off the ground. And worse, assuming people didn't like me because of my mixed race heritage. And then there you were. One of the princesses of the Collingsworth royalty. Beautiful, rich and holding the heart of the boy I loved. Yeah, I think it's pretty safe to say I hated you."

The words stabbed at Jessa's heart. "But we became friends." She paused. "Didn't we?"

Maura's expression softened. "Yes, we did. Don't believe for a moment that what we have now is anything but genuine. I will admit though, I wasn't completely honest early on."

"What do you mean?"

"When we first worked together that summer, I still didn't like you, even when I found out that you and Lance had broken up. I wanted you to feel the sting of rejection the way I had with Lance, which is why I made sure you knew he had gotten engaged to Daphne and that she was pregnant." Maura's brows drew together. "I felt really bad about that later, especially when they didn't end up getting married."

"They never got married?"

Maura looked at her in surprise. "You didn't know that? I know I didn't tell you when I found out, but I assumed someone told you or that you didn't care. You weren't talking about Lance anymore, so I just let it go."

Jessa struck down the hope that flared to life in her heart. It didn't matter that he hadn't married Daphne. He'd still cheated on her. That was something she couldn't seem to get beyond. "No one ever told me. He'd moved away, and I hadn't been close with anyone who knew him, so I heard nothing more until he showed up with renovation plans in hand and the news Gran had hired him to do the work."

"I guess that was a shock, huh?" Maura asked.

"Yep." Jessa took a sip of her water then said, "But what I want to know is how we ended up being friends if you hated me so much."

"As that summer progressed, I could see how hard you worked for my parents, and my mom let slip one day that you did it all for free. Your help during the startup of their business was what kept them from going under. They didn't have to pay for someone to help, and people loved the designs you did for them. And I also saw the respect you had for my parents. You never treated them with anything but courtesy. That meant a lot to me. I also got to know you and discovered the princess crown you wore wasn't one you wanted. And that you weren't a snob, but just reserved and somewhat shy. All three of you older Collingsworth girls were that way. Cami was probably the only one who took the town by storm without regard for where it landed her."

Jessa laughed. "Yes, she's still that way."

Maura reached across the counter and touched Jessa's hand. "I love you. You taught me so much about myself and how to be a better person. I just hope all this stuff hasn't made you reconsider our friendship."

Jessa looked down at the glass in her hands. "I did wonder, but I just needed to know what had happened back then. I don't think even you are a good enough actor to pull off a friendship while hating a person for this long."

"No, I could never do that. I do hope you'll forgive me for what I thought about you back then."

Jessa slid off the stool and went around the counter to embrace Maura. "We're in this for the long haul. Destined to be best friends in whatever nursing home we end up in."

As they laughed together, Jessa felt relief replace the burden she'd been carrying since her talk with Lance the night before.

After looking through the millions of pictures Maura had taken on her trip, Jessa headed back to the manor. She had just pulled to a stop in front of the garage when her cell phone rang.

She answered it as she got out of the car.

"Jessa? It's Dean."

"Hi, Dean." Jessa walked toward the trailer, phone pressed to her ear. "What can I do for you?"

"Is Violet around there?"

"I'm not sure. I just got back from town." She opened the door of the trailer and stepped into its cool interior. A quick glance revealed it to be empty. "She's not in the trailer, but she might be in the house. Is something wrong with her cell?"

Dean paused. "No. I think she's just not taking my calls."

Jessa sank down on the end of her bed. "What happened?"

"I'm not entirely sure, to be honest," Dean said. "She came into town, and we had a late lunch together. Just before I went back to work, I reminded her I'd be gone for Monday and Tuesday next week."

"That shouldn't have upset her," Jessa commented.

"I know. We'd discussed it briefly before, so she knew about it. I'm going to a conference in Chicago, but would be home Wednesday afternoon."

"Is Addy staying here with us or is Violet going to stay with her at your place?" There was a long silence. "Dean?"

"Neither. I'm having Miss Sylvia take care of her."

"Why wouldn't you ask Violet to stay with her? They adore each other."

"I don't know. I'm just so used to Miss Sylvia watching her, plus with all the renovations I figured she'd be in the way."

"And did you explain that to Violet when you told her Addy was going to be with Sylvia?"

"No." Dean's sigh was audible even over the phone. "Do you think that's what has upset her?"

"I'm not sure it would upset her, but it might have made her wonder if you really do trust her with Addy."

"I never meant to do that. She didn't say anything, but after she left, I kind of got the feeling she wasn't happy. I thought it was because I was going away. But now that she's not even answering my calls..."

Jessa flopped back on the bed, glad to be focusing on someone else's relationship problems instead of her own.

"How do you really feel about her?"

"What do you mean?"

"Do you see yourself having a future with her?" Jessa wondered, however, as she asked the question if she was in any position to be giving Dean relationship advice.

"Of course. I hope we get married and grow old together."

"And she knows this?"

"I would hope so. I tell her I love her all the time. And I do. More than I ever thought possible."

Jessa heard the catch in Dean's voice as he said the words and swallowed hard. Would a guy ever feel so strongly about her? "Are you planning to propose to her any time soon?"

"We haven't known each other that long," Dean pointed out. "It's only been about three months since we first met."

"So you're not proposing because it's too soon, even though you know you want to spend the rest of your life with her?"

Dean sighed again. "Something like that."

"That's ridiculous, Dean," Jessa said bluntly. "If you already know you love her and want to spend the rest of your life with her, why wait? Neither of you is getting any younger. But, at the very least, I think you should have Violet take care of Addy for the two days you are gone. I'm guessing she might be wondering if you're not sure about her ability to be a wife and mother. Which is no doubt feeding into her own doubts about that."

"Why would she have doubts about being a good wife and mother?" Dean asked. "I've never suggested that to her."

"You don't have to. All of us girls wonder that. We didn't have the greatest examples growing up, so we wonder if we'll be able to parent at all given how our own mother abandoned us, and Gran...well, Gran tried, but she really wasn't the mother we needed."

"I never realized..." Dean's words trailed off.

"Laurel is giving us some hope that maybe we can move past the way we were raised to have happy, healthy relationships, but it's hard to lose the doubts and insecurities."

"I understand." And Jessa could hear from the firm tone of his voice that he did. "I think I know where she's gone if she's not around there."

"Don't give up on her, Dean," Jessa said. "She deserves to be loved the way you love her. I want only happiness for the two of you."

"I think it's time I did what my heart's been telling me to do for a while instead of worrying about what people would think."

"Excellent idea," Jessa agreed. "Besides, the only person who would truly object to things happening too soon isn't here anymore. Follow your heart."

"Thanks, Jessa."

After the call ended, Jessa lay there staring up at the ceiling. Every word she'd said to Dean had been true, although she wasn't sure how much applied to Cami. She wasn't altogether sure Cami even wanted to be a wife or mother. But Jessa knew that personally, in the well protected part of her heart, it was her greatest longing and deepest fear. She knew she could be reserved and wasn't the most affectionate person around. Would she never be able to connect emotionally with a man? Would her reserve make her a bad mother?

She curled onto her side and closed her eyes. Remembering how things had ended with Lance and then later with Aaron, Jessa wondered if it was even possible for a man to care enough about her to take the time to get past the protective shell she'd placed around her heart.

Please, God, take this longing from me. I don't want to feel that hurt once more. I'd much rather not have to be that vulnerable ever again.

"Jessa? Are you here?"

"Yes. In here," Jessa said as she sat up.

Cami stepped through the doorway. "Lance is looking for you."

"What does he want?" Jessa slid off the side of the bed and stretched.

"He said something about arrangements to go pick out some cabinets."

Jessa sighed. "I don't suppose you'd be interested in a trip to Fargo."

Cami shook her head. "Absolutely not. The cute guys are here. And besides, this isn't going to be my house, so I could care less about what the cabinets look like."

"This will always be your home, Cam," Jessa said. She walked around the end of the bed and into the main area of the trailer with Cami.

"It's never really felt like home to me. Maybe all that," Cami waved her hand in the direction of the manor, "will change things, but I'm not holding my breath."

A rap on the door of the trailer drew Jessa's attention. She glanced at Cami who just shrugged and turned to go to the other end of the trailer where her bed was.

Jessa opened the door, not at all surprised to find Lance there. She tried to ignore the little flip her heart did when she saw him. It was becoming a far too frequent occurrence. When she stepped onto the first step, he moved back, giving her room to exit the trailer.

She crossed her arms over her waist. "Cami said you were looking for me?"

Chapter Fourteen

LANCE nodded. “Any chance we can take that trip into Fargo tomorrow?”

“So soon?” Jessa had hoped for a few more days before having to go with him.

Lance shoved his hands into the pockets of his jeans. “Yes, the sooner, the better. Plus I want to stop by my office real quick.”

Against her better judgment, Jessa found herself agreeing. She still hoped she could convince Violet or maybe Lily to go along for the ride. “What time do you want to leave?”

“Early. Like around seven?”

“I’ll be ready.” Jessa glanced toward the manor as a group of men came out and headed to the trucks parked near the garage. “Everyone done for the day?”

Lance nodded. “Day two is in the books. Things are going well, but I wanted to let you know about another project we are starting tomorrow. It’s one I think you and your sisters can help out with better than the stuff going on inside the house right now."

"What's that?" Jessa looked back at Lance. Her mouth went dry when his intense blue gaze focused in on her.

"Your grandmother was very specific about wanting a gazebo built in the wooded area on the other side of the manor."

Jessa looked to where he pointed. "Why did she want that?"

"I'm not sure, she was just very insistent and had the area marked clearly where she wanted me to dig to build it."

"Dig? Aren't those things usually built above the ground?"

"Yep, but she had a clear plan of what she wanted. A very sturdy structure with a poured concrete base to it."

Jessa shook her head. "I don't know what she would be thinking having that built."

"Well, she did mention something about it being a great place to enjoy nature and to hold weddings."

"Weddings?" Jessa was beginning to wonder if Gran had been slightly off her rocker near the end. None of these plans sounded like something Gran would have wanted.

"I don't care what you guys decide to use it for. All I know is that there are very specific things I have to do in order to get paid for this job, so I'm going to do them. Tomorrow we break ground on the gazebo and will pour the foundation. Once we begin to build it, I figure that's where you ladies will be able to help more."

"Sounds good, I guess. I'm assuming I can't object to any of these plans?"

Lance lifted a brow at her question. "Are you wanting to?"

"Well, this gazebo one seems a little weird and unnecessary. I don't see the sense in it. Weddings?"

Lance shrugged. "I wish I could give your objections more weight, but honestly, I need this to go exactly according to your grandmother's plans."

Jessa frowned. She didn't like being told she had basically no control over what was being done to the manor. While Cami might not view it as her home, Jessa most certainly did. "I'm not going to stop questioning things that make no sense to me."

Lance smiled, his dimples deepening. "I wouldn't expect anything less."

Out of the corner of her eye, Jessa saw people headed their way. She turned and saw it was Matt, Josh and Will, their long strides making quick work of the distance between the manor and the trailers. "Guess it will be time for supper soon."

Matt went right to his trailer while Josh and Will headed in their direction. Jessa still struggled to view Will as a brother, not because she didn't like him, but she really knew him no better than she did Josh.

"Did the day end well?" Lance asked as they came to a stop next to him.

Josh nodded. "No problems today. I had to get after a couple of guys about safety issues. I have made note of warnings issued, and they are aware that subsequent issues could result in loss of work."

Lance nodded. "I won't be around much tomorrow. Jessa and I are going to head into Fargo to order all the things needed. Did the guys get the measurements done?"

"Yep. I have that all for you."

Lance turned to the younger man. "How do you like the work, Will?"

"I'm really enjoying it. I've done a bit of construction work in the past, but this is definitely diving into the deep end."

"Don't feel you have to put in the hours of all the other guys," Lance said.

"I'm happy to do it," Will said with a smile. "I'm here to work."

"Well, don't forget to spend some time with your sisters, too."

"And your grandmother," Jessa added. "I'm sure Sylvia would like to spend a bit of time with you as well."

Will nodded. "I figured I could do that on the weekend. And see if she needs help with anything."

"Dinner in thirty!" Jessa looked over as Laurel called out to them from the doorway of her trailer.

"We'd better clean up," Will said and headed for Lance's RV.

Lance turned back to Jessa and said, "See you at supper." Then he and Josh headed in the direction Will had taken.

Her gaze following them, Jessa couldn't keep from remembering another time she'd watched him walk away from her. The time he'd broken her heart. It was a good thing to remember. Given what the next day held, it was better she focus on the pain he'd caused her rather than the times he'd held her hand tightly in his. Or put his arm around her shoulders as they'd explored the wooded paths surrounding the lake. Or how he'd been her first kiss.

Swallowing hard, Jessa willed her thoughts to stop moving in the direction they were headed. She walked to Laurel's trailer and knocked. "Need any help?"

Laurel opened the door to let her in. "Sure."

"Smells good," Jessa commented. "Spaghetti?"

"Yep. Hope everyone likes it."

"I know I will. Just the fact that I didn't have to cook it is enough for me to love it," Jessa assured her with a smile.

At Laurel's instruction, Jessa joined Rose at the table to help her put a salad together. "Have you seen Violet?"

Laurel turned from the stove. "No. Why?"

"Dean was looking for her earlier. I think they hit a small bump in their romance."

"Ugh. Hope it's nothing too serious."

"I think Dean was going to get it straightened out." Jessa took the cucumber Rose had peeled and began to cut it.

The door to the bedroom at the other end of the trailer opened, and Matt stepped out. He wore a black T-shirt and cutoff jeans, his hair still damp from his shower. "Hey, Jessa."

Jessa returned his greeting and watched as he approached Laurel. He laid a hand on the small of her back and pressed a kiss to the top of her head.

"Well, you smell much better," Laurel commented as she lifted her head. This time he placed a lingering kiss on her lips.

"How's the little one today?" Matt asked as he leaned down to press his cheek to Laurel's belly.

Jessa watched as he caressed the small bump, not even aware of the swell of emotion within her until she had to swallow hard. This was really the first relationship she'd seen up close that had been so affectionate and loving. It was a joy to watch, but it had brought to life a longing deep within her for something like they had.

"Let me do that for you, babe," Matt said when she moved to grasp the handles of the large pot sitting on the stove.

Laurel stepped back and handed him the potholders. "The strainer is in the sink."

Jessa watched them work together to get the noodled strained and ready to serve. She was so glad things had worked out for them. The love and affection they had for each other was clear, and she was pretty sure the baby would only add to that love in the same way having Rose join their family had.

"Rosie, why don't you go tell the others it's time to eat," Matt suggested.

The little girl scampered out of the trailer, leaving Jessa to finish the salad. Cami appeared fairly quickly followed by the men and Rose.

"Where's Lily?" Jessa asked.

"She went into town with her friends," Cami said then glanced around. "Violet still not back?"

"No," Jessa said. "But I think she'll be back a bit later. We don't need to wait for her."

After grace was said for the meal, Jessa waved the others to go ahead while she remained seated, her thoughts on Lily. She had been distracted by so many things lately Jessa realized she was losing touch with the girl. She was gone more than she was around these days. It was a difficult spot to be in. With her having turned eighteen, Jessa knew Lily considered herself an adult, but she wasn't sure she could trust the young woman to make wise decisions in certain areas of her life. She was going to have to make some time to talk with her in the next few days.

"You going to eat?"

Jessa looked up to see Lance standing near the table, a plateful of spaghetti in his hand.

"Yep," Jessa said as she stood up.

"Is everything okay?" Lance asked as she began to put food on her plate.

She glanced at him. "Yes. Why?"

"You looked like you were deep in thought over something."

"Just thinking about Lily. Sometimes I forget what it was like to be that age. Hopefully she's not as naïve as I was," Jessa commented, well aware that Lance would likely pick up on the underlying meaning of her statement.

Lance's gaze narrowed briefly. "I think she's got a good head on her shoulders. You certainly did."

Too bad a good head on her shoulders hadn't been what

he'd wanted back then. "Gran made sure of that. Unfortunately, she didn't have the same influence on Lily. I still haven't decided if that's a good or bad thing."

Once she had her food, Jessa picked up a drink and headed for the door which Lance opened for her. The others had already gathered around the two picnic tables that now stood end to end. Jessa found a spot next to Will while Lance sat across the table from her. Jess wished she could read his mind because she was having a difficult time trying to figure out the signals he was sending. Was he really interested in her? And why now? If she hadn't been enough for him back then, why would she be now?

"You're finished with college?" Jessa asked Will, determined to learn more about this young man who shared her blood.

Will nodded. "Yes. I graduated last year with a degree in business administration."

"Did you have to take time off from a job to come here?"

"No. I haven't started a job yet. I just returned from a year as a short term missionary."

"Really? What exactly did you do?"

"I helped build schools, dig wells, fix orphanages and anything else that needed doing."

"Well, that certainly prepared you for this," Jessa commented. "Where did you go?"

"I was in the Republic of Burundi working with a mission there."

"Africa?" Lance asked. "Josh grew up in Kenya."

Jessa looked at the man seated next to Lance, who nodded in response to Lance's comment.

"Do you speak Swahili?" Will asked.

Josh nodded. "Not as well as I used to though. It's been many years since I last used it."

Will spoke a couple of phrases in a language which Jessa assumed was Swahili. A wide smile crossed Josh's face as he replied to Will. It was the first time Jessa had seen Josh as something other than serious and reserved. She glanced at Cami, wondering if her younger sister noticed Josh's animated response. Sure enough, her sister's gaze was tight on the man. Jessa looked back and forth between Will and Josh as they conversed for a couple of minutes in a language none of the rest of them understood.

"You speak very well," Josh commented in English.

"My parents told me that if I was going to spend a year living among the people in Burundi that I needed to make sure I spoke their language. So I immersed myself as much as I could in their culture. I lived with a local family, and they were more than happy to teach me to speak Swahili even though they all spoke English."

"Not many your age would commit to something like that."

This was the most Jessa had heard Josh talk outside of conversations regarding the renovations.

"I'm not sure if the mission field is where the Lord is calling me, but I wanted to have the experience before I started a career. I'm very glad I took that year to see what life is like for people in one of the poorest countries of the world. Definitely gave me a perspective I would never have gained otherwise."

As Jessa listened to him talk, she realized how...normal he sounded. Like he had none of the messed up baggage the rest of them carried. From the sounds of things, he'd had a mother and father who had encouraged him to follow his dreams and had supported him in every way. So different from how Gran had treated them. She'd been angry when Violet had left and upset when Laurel chose to go to college in Minneapolis instead of Collingsworth. And livid was the only word Jessa could think of to describe Gran's reaction to Cami's abrupt departure to pursue a music career in New York City. Each of them had had to struggle against the tide of disapproval to find their way in the world. She had probably faced the least disapproval simply because she'd chosen a path that hadn't taken her away from Gran and Collingsworth.

They were just finishing their meal when she heard a vehicle approaching the manor. It didn't take long for Dean and Violet to appear around the corner of the building. Addy was between them, skipping as they approached the group. From the looks on their faces, Jessa could almost guess at the news that was to come.

"Hey!" Violet said as they got closer, a big smile on her face. "We have an announcement we'd like to make."

Before anyone could say anything more, Addy blurted out, "Daddy and Violet are getting married!"

"Really?" Laurel stood up and moved to quickly embrace Violet and then Dean. "I'm so happy for you guys. Let me see the ring!"

Jessa got up and gave Violet a hug. As she hugged Dean, she whispered, "Glad you listened to your heart."

"Thank you for your encouragement," Dean said, his eyes sparkling.

"Your ring is beautiful," Laurel said. "Is this a family heirloom, Dean?"

Dean nodded. "It was my grandmother's ring. My mom gave it to me after meeting Violet for the first time. She said she knew that this time it was going to last, and she wanted Violet to have the ring."

Once Laurel released her hand, Violet came and hugged Jessa again. "Thank you. Dean told me he had talked with you."

"I just want you two to be happy." Jessa blinked rapidly as her eyes blurred with tears. "I'm so glad you've found your love."

Violet reached up and brushed a tear from her cheek, her brown eyes also damp. "You'll find yours too, Jess. Just let

God work in your heart and keep an open mind."

As the others congratulated them, Jessa returned to her spot at the table and picked up her plate and cup. She was perilously close to bursting into tears. The last thing she wanted was for that to happen in front of Lance. Not that she wanted it to happen at all. She hated it when her emotions got the better of her. Inside the trailer, she put her plate in the garbage and then took the time to fill her cup with more water. She stood with her hip braced against the counter, her back to the door and took several deep breaths. It didn't take long for her emotions to settle and the tears in her eyes to dry up.

"Everything okay?"

The sound of Lance's voice threatened to unsettle her again, but Jessa took a quick breath, blew it out and then turned to face him. "Yes." She forced herself to hold his gaze, all the while working to keep any emotion from her face. "It's about time Dean popped the question."

"About time? They haven't known each other that long, have they?" Lance asked.

Jessa shrugged. "Sometimes you just know. Time isn't a factor."

Before Lance could reply to that, the door to the trailer opened and Laurel came in. When she saw Lance she smiled, but then said, "Out you go. Too many people in here."

Lance looked her way, then, with a nod at Laurel, left the trailer. Laurel set down the dishes she was carrying and began to sort them into the garbage and sink. "You doing okay?"

"I'm fine. Just emotional over the happy news. I suspected he was going to propose to her and still it choked me up."

"I'm glad they finally got to this point. Though it does sound funny to say finally since it hasn't really been that long."

"And yet it feels like they've been together forever. Like they were meant to be."

Laurel nodded. "Wonder when they'll set the wedding date?"

The trailer door opened again, and this time it was Violet who came in, Cami behind her. "What are you two doing in here?"

"Making wedding plans," Laurel said. "I think we should wear those big ballroom style dresses. In bright colors."

"You'd better be joking," Cami said as she flopped down on the couch. "You'd have to drag me down the aisle if that's what we have to wear."

"I think it's a great idea," Violet said. "But I do want you all in the same color. Since I'm partial to the outdoors, I think I'd like them to be bright green."

Jessa lifted a brow at Violet. "Well, in my opinion you should just have a small intimate ceremony with no bridesmaids at all."

Violet started to laugh. "That's actually probably closer to what we'll do." She held up a hand. "I promise there will be no ballroom dresses in bright green. Or any other colors."

Glad for the light conversation, Jessa moved to dry the few non-disposable dishes that Laurel had washed in the small sink. "Well, maybe you can get married in the new gazebo Gran made Lance promise to build."

"What gazebo?" Laurel asked as she handed her the salad bowl.

Jessa shared what Lance had told her about the new building project. "He doesn't know why she wanted it, but he's going to build it because if he doesn't, he won't get all the money from the project."

Violet shrugged. "I don't suppose it would harm anything to have one built."

After the dishes were all done, the ladies went back

outside with the dessert Laurel had prepared.

Unlike the previous night, once the dessert was finished, people helped clean up and then went their separate ways without lingering for conversation. Violet and Cami came with Jessa to the trailer.

"So, any chance you want to take a trip to Fargo tomorrow, Vi?" Jessa asked as she settled down on the couch.

Violet shook her head. "I'm not really into the home decor stuff."

"You don't have to make any decisions. Just come for the company."

Violet tilted her head to the side, and Jessa worked to keep from looking away. "I think you and Lance should use the time to talk about your past."

"What's to discuss?" Jessa asked. "He broke up with me. We went our separate ways. Nothing to discuss there."

"Okay. Then it would be a good time to catch up with an old friend."

Knowing she'd get no help from Violet, Jessa sighed. "Seriously, guys. I'm not all that anxious to spend six hours on the road with an ex-boyfriend."

No one seemed willing to help her out though, and even Lily turned down her invitation when she got home. Resigned to her fate, Jessa decided to call it a night since the next day was going to start earlier than usual.

ᴄ Chapter Fifteen ᴄ

THE next morning, Lance stood at the front of his truck reading through email on his phone. When he was satisfied nothing would need his attention while on the road, he returned the phone to the holder on his belt and touched the blue tooth earpiece to turn it on.

As seven o'clock approached, he wondered if Jessa was going to show. A couple of minutes later, he watched through his sunglasses as the door to her trailer opened, and she stepped out. She made her way toward him with sure steps. She wore a pair of white capris and a turquoise color blouse that would no doubt accentuate the color of her eyes if they weren't hidden behind a pair of sunglasses not too different from his. Her hair was down in loose curls, and the sun emphasized the blonde and red highlights of it. She had always been the most beautiful woman to him.

"Ready to go?" he asked as she approached.

"Yep." She lifted the travel coffee cup she held. "Have coffee, will travel."

Lance opened the passenger side door for her and waited until she was settled before closing it. He was a little nervous about the trip, so as he rounded the front of the truck to get behind the wheel, he prayed that it would go smoothly. He wanted a chance to explain the past, but didn't want to push it on her.

Silence held the cab of the truck in its grip as he drove away from the manor and out onto the highway. To make it a little less awkward, Lance turned on the stereo. The gospel music CD he'd been listening to filled the air.

"I know this group," Jessa commented. "Gran used to listen to them all the time. They broke up, didn't they? I went looking for their latest recent for a birthday present for Gran one year, but couldn't find anything. The clerk at the Christian bookstore said something about the group disbanding."

Lance contemplated revealing what he knew about the group and its demise but that was Josh's story to tell, not his. "Yes. The group broke up almost eight years ago."

"That's too bad. Gran really liked their style and how they sang the old hymns and gospel songs she knew."

"Yes, they were certainly a group with a bright future." Lance sensed her gaze on him, and when he took his eyes off the road briefly, he saw he was right.

"You must have been a big fan if you still listen to them. I don't remember you being all that big into gospel music when we...were in high school."

"I wasn't, but I kind of have a personal connection with this group."

"Really? You knew someone in the group."

"Yep. Josh was the lead singer."

There was a beat of silence then Jessa said, "Josh? Like your cousin Josh?"

"The very same. He was big into music and started the quartet up while he was in college. I didn't know him too well back then because he was living in Nashville at the time."

"So what happened? How did Josh end up working with your business?"

Again Lance hesitated, not sure how much to reveal of Josh's past. Josh had never tried to hide what had occurred, but he wasn't one to discuss it much either. "There were some lapses in moral judgment that forced the group to disband. The Christian community was quick to turn their backs on the people involved, and that was the death knell for them." Jessa didn't say anything in response to his statement, so he added, "And to answer the question you're probably trying to decide whether or not to ask, yes, Josh was involved."

"I'm sure that was a very difficult time for him."

"Yes. There were a lot of things happening at the same time that clouded the whole issue, much of which people never knew all the details of. Josh went through hell. Yes, some of it was of his own making, but some wasn't. In the end, he was a shattered man with no place to go. I invited him to come help me until he could figure out what he wanted to do with his life. He showed up seven years ago and hasn't left. And I hope he never does. He's my right hand. I don't know what I'd do without him."

"I never would have guessed that about Josh," Jessa said. "But I don't really know him."

"He comes across shy, kinda like you," Lance said with a smile. "But the reality is, he is cautious around people because in the past, those he trusted hurt him the most."

"I know that feeling," Jessa remarked quietly.

Lance's stomach clenched at her words. No doubt he was one of the people who had hurt her in the past. He gripped the steering wheel tightly, trying to decide if now was the time to broach the subject. It seemed to be an opening for him, so he took it. "I know I was one who hurt you, Jess. I'm very sorry about that."

"What's done is done," she replied in an emotionless slightly muffled voice.

Lance glanced at her as he reached to turn down the music and saw that this time she had turned away from him and was staring out the side window. "Yes, it's done, but that doesn't mean I don't owe you an apology for how it happened."

"How else could it have happened?" she asked. "It's not like there are too many ways to dump someone. Well, I suppose you could have done it on the phone or in an email."

"Just so you know, ending our relationship was the hardest thing I've ever done." He wasn't sure she'd believe that his heart had been as broken as hers when it had happened. "But I felt like I had no other choice."

Jessa didn't respond, and Lance wondered if that was the end of the conversation. But then she said, "I know about Daphne."

"What?"

"I know about her being pregnant and you two getting engaged."

Lance was speechless for a moment. "Well, in the end I couldn't go through with the marriage and thankfully, when she miscarried, it meant I didn't have to."

"How can you be thankful for a miscarriage?" Jessa asked. "That was your child that was lost."

Lance shot her a glance. "My child? No, the baby wasn't mine."

"It wasn't? Then why were you going to marry her?"

Lance didn't reply right away. He was still trying to absorb the notion that she thought he'd cheated on her. "It was Dave's. He and Daphne had had an on again, off again relationship for a couple of years. After their last breakup, before she found out she was pregnant, he took off. She was beside herself being pregnant and not married, so I agreed to marry her since Dave wasn't around. Besides, at that point, I figured if I couldn't be with you, then it didn't matter who I was with."

"But why did you think you couldn't you be with me?"

He tried to pull his scattered thoughts together. He had assumed she knew things that she didn't, and he hadn't realized she'd known other things. "I couldn't be with you because your grandmother told me I couldn't. She came to me and told me I had to end things with you. She gave me fifty-thousand dollars to leave you alone. I tried to say no, but she told me that if I didn't do it voluntarily, she'd make sure it happened anyway. I didn't know what else to do, so I took the money."

"She paid you? And you took it?"

"If I was going to lose you anyway, I was going to make your grandmother pay," Lance said, remembering the anger that had coursed through him back then. "And the sad truth was my family needed the money. Dad had had to move to Fargo early to start his job and then Mom was diagnosed with cancer. She needed money for medicines and other things until Dad's insurance kicked in. I tried to make the best out of a bad situation. Then just after Mom and I moved to Fargo, Daphne told us she was pregnant. It was a horrible time all around."

"I wish I had known all that, but I do know what Gran meant when she said that she'd make it happen regardless." Lance felt Jessa shift in her seat. "I just found a letter from Gran the other day that she'd written to me explaining something about us. She didn't mention anything about her conversations with you though. She just told me why she thought, at that time, things couldn't work out between us anyway."

"What did she mean?" Lance asked. He had always wondered about what it was she had threatened to reveal. He'd thought about challenging her back then, but between his dad's job, his mother's diagnosis, and moving away, the chance to help his family weighed heavily on him. Not to mention he had been a little afraid to take on the Collingsworth matriarch. He'd heard rumors over the years about her ruthlessness if you crossed her. He couldn't risk having his family in her crosshairs.

As he listened to Jessa explain about the possibility of them being cousins, he was suddenly very glad he'd taken the money and not forced Julia to show her hand. Had accusations like that come out against his uncle—even though he'd heard rumors over the years—it would have been overwhelming for his father. To deal with a wife having cancer, a move, a new job and a brother charged with statutory rape...it might have been too much for him. "So the test proved that we weren't related?"

"Yes. The test she had run on my DNA and your uncle's came back with no possibility of us being related."

"So maybe your grandmother saw hiring me as a way to make up for what happened back then?"

"It's possible." Jessa sighed. "I'm finding out I know a lot less about my grandmother than I thought I did. Too many secrets."

He glanced over at her in time to see her look down at the purse in her lap. "Do you think there are more secrets yet that you don't know about?"

"Yes, I do. At one time, I would never have believed Gran would have hidden so many things. But after finding out about Will... Well, anything is possible."

"I'm sure that must have been difficult," Lance said.

"It was at first, but now I'm more resigned than anything. I'm pretty sure there's still at least one more big secret out there. The one pertaining to where our mother is now. Violet's been digging, but hasn't been able to find anything. I have a feeling the reason is that Gran had a hand in hiding that information. No doubt she was able to pay people off along the way."

"Are you interested in knowing what happened to your mom?" Lance asked. As a teenager, she hadn't spoken at all about the woman and had dismissed his questions about her. He wondered if it would be the same this time around.

"I wasn't," Jessa said. "But with Violet digging around, I figure it's inevitable something will turn up. I'm a little more curious, but not too interested in a relationship with her."

"Why's that?" Lance was banking on her being more interested in not discussing their past so she'd answer these questions about her mom.

"I never understood why she did what she did. I mean I get that you can make a bad decision once, but six times? With five different men? I know she and Gran never got along, but that didn't mean she had to go out and keep having kids. Especially when she had no interest in raising them."

"Five different men?" Lance asked.

"Yes. Cami and Laurel have the same father. I guess he hung around long enough to get her knocked up twice."

"Sometimes there is just no understanding," Lance said. "I've had a few situations like that in my life. In the end, I just had to let it go and commit the situation and the people involved to the Lord. It's entirely possible she herself doesn't understand what she does."

"I've worried about Cami going down that same road. She missed out on the teen pregnancy and so far seems to be smart enough to keep from getting knocked up now. But like our mother, she wants to get a big break in the music industry. I'm concerned she is compromising her self-worth to get it." Jessa paused. "And yes, I do get frustrated with her for the same reasons. I just don't understand the way she acts. A little flirting, sure, but she goes beyond that. I hate to think of the trouble she's gotten into because of her drinking."

"Again, probably not much you can do except pray for her."

"I'd much rather lock her in a room where she can't make any decisions that would harm her," Jessa commented. "But I'd hate to put Dean in the position of having to arrest me for forcibly confining her. Even if it was for her own good."

Surprised to hear a hint of humor in her words, Lance glanced at Jessa and saw a small smile on her face. "That's the problem with having a law enforcement officer as part of the family."

"Yep. But I think he'll be a good addition."

"Matt seems like a good guy as well."

"He is. He and Laurel went through a rough patch over the past few weeks, but thankfully they were able to work it out. With her being pregnant and now claiming Rose as her own, I'm so glad they didn't lose each other."

"Are they thinking of moving back to Collingsworth?"

"I'm not sure. They haven't said anything. We each received an inheritance from Gran that would mean they could move wherever they wanted and not have to work if they spent their money wisely. However, Matt doesn't strike me as the type who would want to just sit around and do nothing. So unless he found a job here, I think they're going to stay in Minneapolis."

"I might have a possibility for that."

"Really? Something with your company?"

Lance nodded. "In the two days I've worked with him I can already see he would be a good addition to the company. He isn't afraid to get his hands dirty, and the guys on the job respect him. And even better, he and Josh seem to work well together. It was just a thought I had and wondered if they'd ever said anything about moving back."

"It would be rather amazing if we all ended up back in Collingsworth. Well, maybe not all. I still can't picture Cami being happy here, but I think Laurel would be, especially if it meant she didn't have to make Rose switch schools."

"I may broach the subject with Matt nearer the end of the week and see what he thinks. Don't say anything though, please."

"You're asking me to keep a secret?" Jessa asked.

Lance chuckled. "Just for a few days. Not forever, I promise."

As his truck ate up the miles between Collingsworth and Fargo, Lance answered the questions Jessa asked regarding his company and how it had gotten started. He was glad she was willing to talk, even if it wasn't about their past, present or possible future. Knowing now what she had thought about what had transpired around the time of their breakup, it was no wonder he'd received such a chilly response when he'd showed up. Not only had she had to deal with their breakup, she had to deal with what she assumed was his cheating on her.

Would knowing the truth make any difference for her now? Lance hoped it would, because he saw so much of the girl he'd fallen in love with mixed in with the maturity she'd gained over the years. All of it a very attractive package to him.

They approached Moorhead just before ten and drove into the parking lot of the first place in Fargo he wanted to stop at a short time later. He had three places he hoped they could fit in during this trip. The easiest ones would be first-appliances and flooring. The last place would be the one where they would choose the cabinets for the kitchen along with countertop and tiling.

He hoped it wouldn't be an overwhelming process, but he knew it could be if a person were indecisive at all. From what he remembered of Jessa, she wasn't that type of person, but only time would tell today.

It didn't take Jessa long at all to settle on the appliances she wanted. He was pretty sure she'd done some research before this trip because she had specific questions for the sales person and seemed knowledgeable about the features of each unit she considered. Lance was happy to sit back and let her decide this. There would be more limitations in the selections to come, so he wasn't going to limit her here.

At the flooring place, they had their first difference of opinion, but once again, Jessa seemed to have done her research and presented him with a well thought out defense of why she wanted a certain type of flooring in a couple of the rooms. She may not have had much say in the plans for the house and things that her grandmother had made sure were not optional, but she was making up for it now.

"Want to go for lunch first, or hit up the final place we need to go to?" Lance asked as they walked out of the flooring store.

"Let's finish up with the stores," Jessa replied, lifting a hand to capture her hair as a gust of wind swept by them.

Not too surprised, by her decision, Lance opened the door of his truck, and the warmth of the day turned to a blast of heat from the cab. He laid a hand on Jessa's arm as she moved to get in. "Let it cool just a second. The downside to a black truck."

Jessa nodded as a small smile lifted one corner of her mouth. "A minor inconvenience for you, I'm sure."

"Well, I do need a truck for my job. Always hauling stuff around, you know.

She quirked an eyebrow at him. "Like a fifth wheel? Or a boat?"

He chuckled, glad to see a flash of her sense of humor. "Well, yes. Those too."

After touching the upholstery, Jessa said, "I think it's safe now." She grabbed the handle on the roof above the door and pulled herself up into the seat.

Lance found himself smiling as he went around to the driver's side. So far, barring the first few revelations, the day had gone well, even better than he had dared hope. But, he reminded himself, the day still wasn't over. He wouldn't count it a success until they'd done everything they'd come to accomplish, they were back at the manor, and she was still talking to him.

The cabinet place took longer than the other two places, but she was still fairly quick in her decisions. It was clear she had a good idea of what she did and didn't want. Dismissing things she didn't like with a wave of her hand, she would run her fingertips over cabinet fronts and countertops that seemed to appeal to her.

Lance let her work with the sales person who helped her decide on how she wanted the kitchen to look based on the measurements he had provided. He interjected a few comments when necessary as it pertained to the structure of the kitchen and what wouldn't work. She argued over a few things with him, but by and large she accepted the restrictions he laid out.

Still, he breathed a sigh of relief when she gave her final approval to the layout of the kitchen and everything that went with it. He had thought of insisting she use an interior decorator to help with the plans, but he could see now that probably wouldn't have worked too well. She definitely had her ideas about what she wanted the manor to look like when it was all said and done.

"Let's grab a bite to eat and head over to my office before we hit the road," Lance suggested as they left the store.

Jessa agreed, and Lance decided to take her to Kroll's Diner, a restaurant he enjoyed visiting, though usually he brought his niece and nephew. It was nothing fancy, but the food was good, and the ambiance inside the restaurant that was set up like a 50's style diner was fun. And there was nothing remotely romantic about it, so Lance hoped she wouldn't find it uncomfortable.

ᴇ Chapter Sixteen ᴓ

*J*ESSA glanced around the restaurant as she stepped inside with Lance right behind her. His choice surprised her, but she found herself liking the look of the place. The hostess seated them right away and left them to peruse the menus. Lance offered some suggestions that made it obvious this wasn't his first time to eat there.

After they'd placed their orders, Jessa sat back in the booth and looked out the large glass window next to her. It looked out over the parking lot, so not a great view, but at least it kept her from staring at the man sitting across from her. She wasn't sure what to say to Lance. The revelations that had come on the drive from Collingsworth were front and center in her mind now that she wasn't focused on decisions for the manor. Finding out he hadn't cheated on her had been somewhat startling. Had Maura known the true details of Daphne's pregnancy?

While she understood why Lance had done what he had and even what had motivated Gran, Jessa still couldn't shake the feeling that everything came down to money with him. Money had been the enticement to get him to leave her, and it was once again what Gran had used to get him back into her life. One would think that if she really had meant that much to him, he would have sought her out before now. It wouldn't have been difficult to find out if she still lived in Collingsworth and was still single. But instead it had taken Gran offering him the job of a lifetime in order to get him back into her life.

"Are you okay?" Lance asked.

Jessa looked at him, meeting his gaze directly. "I'm fine. Just a lot to take in today." She debated beating around the bush, but that wasn't her style, and it would just confuse things if it wasn't all laid out clearly. "Are you wanting to try to rekindle what we had as teenagers?"

Lance's eyes widened but then he smiled. "Well, you were always straight to the point, weren't you?"

Jessa didn't return his smile. She wasn't sure how she felt about his answer. "I'm too old to be beating around the bush with this kind of stuff."

The smile faded from Lance's face. "I'm not sure. What I do know is that I haven't been able to connect with a woman since you. I tried. Both times it got even close to serious, the women broke it off because they felt I wasn't totally all in with the relationship. I think I've always wondered how we might have turned out because I didn't want to end things with you. It was forced on me and on you. I tried to move on, but when I saw you again... Well, there's just a need inside me to know for sure if there is or isn't something still there between us."

"And if I'm not interested?" Jessa asked.

Lance regarded her, his blue eyes narrowed. "Say the word, and I won't be a bother anymore."

"The thing is, I'm trying to wrap my mind around the fact that money is tied up in all of this."

Lance sat back. "What do you mean?"

"You dumped me for money the first time around, and now here you are again because of the money Gran offered you for this job." Jessa paused then said, "What would you say if I told you I'd only consider a relationship with you if you agreed to do this job for cost and nothing more?"

Shock crossed Lance's face. "What?"

"You take enough money to cover the cost of this project—labor and parts—but no profit."

Lance opened his mouth then closed it again. Before he could respond, the waitress showed up with their food. Jessa suddenly had no appetite, and by the look of it, Lance didn't either. She felt a pang of remorse for the harsh way she'd approached things. It was how she felt, but she could have been a little less blunt about it.

Lance's phone rang, and he looked relieved for the interruption as he answered it.

"What's wrong?" he said after greeting Josh.

Jessa wished she could hear the other side of the conversation because clearly Lance was concerned.

"Okay. Stop all work in that area. We're on our way back. And I guess you'd better have someone call Dean."

Worry flared to life at the mention of Dean's name. It was never good to have to call the sheriff.

"We need to go," Lance said as he ended the call. He lifted his hand and motioned the waitress over.

She frowned at the sight of the plates not touched. "Is something wrong with the food?"

Lance shook his head. "We've had an emergency come up. Could you package this up and bring the bill right away?"

The waitress nodded and whisked both plates up and headed for the kitchen.

"What's happened?" Jessa asked as Lance pulled out his wallet and took out a couple of bills and laid them on the table.

"That was Josh. He said they started to dig the gazebo

foundation and discovered a body.”

Jessa stared at Lance in shock. “A body?”

Lance nodded. “We’ll talk more in the truck.”

The waitress was back quickly and set the containers down on the table. She handed the bill to Lance, who glanced at it then gave it back to her along with the money he’d pulled from his wallet. “Keep the change.”

Fighting a sick feeling in her stomach, Jessa followed him from the restaurant to the truck. He didn’t say anything as he put the truck in gear and exited the parking lot. If she hadn’t been so worried, Jessa would have asked him to slow down, but Lance appeared to press the speed limit as he wove in and out of traffic. Once they were headed east on the highway to Collingsworth, he finally glanced at her.

“Josh said they’d only dug down two or three feet when they came upon a skull. They stopped working, so they don’t know if they whole body is there, but even just the skull is enough for concern.”

Jessa stared out the window. “She knew it was there.”

“What?” She glanced at Lance and found his gaze was moving between her and the road.

“You said Gran was insistent that you build the gazebo there, right?”

“Yes, she was very specific about where she wanted it.”

“Well, I can only assume she knew the body was there and wanted it to be found.”

Lance didn’t say anything, but Jessa knew he saw the logic in her statement. Suddenly a thought occurred to her. Reaching for her purse, she opened it and pulled out the large envelope she’d placed there earlier. She’d kept it close, not wanting anyone to find it by accident. She blew out a breath as she opened it and slid out the still sealed envelope.

“What’s that?”

“Possibly an explanation for this,” Jessa said. “It’s a letter from Gran about our mother. If that is our mom, this will no doubt tell us."

"You think it might be your mom?" Lance sounded horrified at the thought. "Why wouldn't she bury her properly?"

Jessa shrugged. "I have no idea."

She slid a finger under the flap of the envelope to break the seal. Though it was the very last thing she wanted to do, she unfolded the paper and began to read. There was no introduction or emotional words to begin this letter like there had been with the others. It was just straightforward and to the point, starting with the date almost eighteen years earlier.

Elizabeth had come home to bring yet another child, Lily, but she had not come alone. Scott Lewis was with her, and I immediately disliked the man. He was disrespectful to her and to me. I feared for her safety with him more than at any other time in her life. As I had done each time she'd come home with a child to leave, I gave her a sizeable amount of money in order to help her out. I told her not to tell Scott since I had given her the money in cash, but she wouldn't listen.

I heard them fighting later that day. I told Scott he had to leave, but he wouldn't listen to me. It was horrible and frightening. When Scott insisted they leave the manor so they could talk away from me, I took my gun from the safe and followed them. It took me a few minutes to figure out which way they had gone, but I soon heard them in the woods, the fight still going strong. As I approached, the verbal fighting stopped, but I heard Elizabeth cry out. By the time I got to where they were, he had her on the ground and was kicking and punching her. She wasn't moving. I was terrified he had killed her. When he turned and saw me there, I felt I was in danger too, so I shot him. I was still convinced Elizabeth was dead, so I got Jonathan to help me. He came and checked her out and discovered that she was still alive. He helped me load her into the car because he said I could get her to the hospital more quickly than waiting for an ambulance. He then stayed behind to take care of the body after he determined that Scott was, in fact, dead.

They quickly discovered that she needed more care than could be provided at the hospital in Collingsworth, and she was air lifted to Minneapolis. I don't know if you remember Sylvia coming to stay with you while I went on a business trip. That "trip" was to be with your mother. She was so close to death and was on life support. They encouraged me to disconnect it because they said she was brain dead. Finally, after several days with no improvement, I agreed to do just that. Surprisingly, she didn't die but stabilized and improved slightly. At the time of writing this letter, she still lives. Unfortunately, she has never recovered from the beating. I have placed her in a special home with round the clock nursing care.

I have included the information on exactly where she is with this letter. Your mother won't know who you are, but it might help those of you who have wondered about her to be able to visit with her. I paid off the people I had to in order to keep them quiet about the events of that night. I couldn't bear the thought of a trial that would impact you girls when you had no one but me to care for you, so I kept this one last secret. The biggest of them all.

I claim responsibility for all the events of that night. Jonathan acted only at my request as his employer. I have arranged to have the body discovered if this letter isn't opened before the renovations start on the manor. Please forgive me once again, but I did what I felt I had to in order to protect my daughter and to make sure you girls weren't left alone while you were still all so young.

The paper crumpled beneath her fingers as Jessa closed her eyes. Blood pounded through her veins drowning out all sound. Murder. Life support. Still alive. Her breath came in short pants from her lungs as a vice-like feeling came over her chest.

Suddenly she was aware of hands on her arms, turning her, pulling her close. She hadn't even noticed when Lance had pulled the truck over and come around to her side of the vehicle. He'd released her from her seat belt and now held her, his hand stroking her back.

"It will be okay," he murmured against her temple. "Breathe. Just breathe."

Jessa tried to focus on the sound of his voice and did as he instructed. Deep breath in. Slow breath out. Gradually the pounding subsided, and the tightness in her chest eased. She didn't move right away. In his arms, she felt a sense of security that she never had experienced before. And she believed him when he said it would be okay. At least, right then she did.

When she finally felt more in control of herself, Jessa moved back from Lance, realizing as she did that she had been clinging to him as much as he had been holding her. She would take the time later to feel embarrassed about that, but right now there was too much that demanded attention from both of them.

Though no longer holding her, Lance didn't move too far away. He reached out and cupped her chin to raise her head. Once their gazes met, he let go of her chin, his fingers gliding gently across her skin. He pushed his sunglasses onto the top of his head, and she could read the concern in his eyes.

"What was in the letter?" he asked.

"That's not my mom's body," Jessa told him. "It is her boyfriend's. Gran killed him."

Lance's eyes widened. Rather than try to explain it all to him, she handed him the crumpled letter. After staring at her for a second, he looked down at the paper. Jessa turned her gaze out the front window of the truck. Lance had pulled over onto the shoulder, but the truck still shook as a semi passed them on the highway. They needed to get back on the road. Though a part of her didn't want to have to deal with any of this, she knew they had to get back because they both would be involved in how it was handled.

"Wow," Lance said as he handed the paper back to her.

"We'd better get going. We can talk on the road."

Lance nodded and waited for her to turn back around in her seat before he closed the door. He paused at the front of the truck as another semi blasted past them. After he swung up into his seat, he started the engine and pulled back out onto the highway.

They rode in silence for a few miles before he said, "You need to call Violet. Without you there, she is the one most likely having to deal with this."

Jessa nodded. "And I need to call our lawyer too, just so he's aware in case we need legal advice."

"Jessa!" Violet answered on the first ring. "Josh said he phoned to let Lance know what's going on. Are you almost home?"

"We just left Fargo. It's going to be a couple of hours before we're there. Are you okay?"

"No. I'm not okay. They found a body on our property." Her voice cracked as she spoke, and Jessa heard her take a deep breath. "Do you think it's Mom's?"

Glad she could offer that small comfort, Jessa told her about the letter, a stilted written confession as it were. The silence that followed her revelations was heavy with emotion.

"How long have you had the letter?" Violet asked, her voice low and tight.

Jessa swallowed. This was the one question she had hoped Violet wouldn't ask. "I found it while I was cleaning out Gran's rooms."

"So you've had it several days and didn't open it? Or give it to me to open?" Violet demanded. "You're as bad as she was. Keeping secrets when you had no right!"

The call ended with that statement, and Jessa was left

with a knotted stomach and the sick feeling at the truth in her sister's words. She clenched the phone tightly as she lowered her hand to her lap. *You're as bad as she was.* The words were like a slap across her face every time they replayed in her mind.

"Hey," Lance prompted. "What did she say?"

"That I'm as bad as Gran was at keeping things secret." At that moment, as the weight of responsibility descended heavily on her, Jessa understood why her grandmother had kept the secrets she did. Now, as the oldest, the responsibility for the family fell on her shoulders. It was hard to not want to do what she could to keep this discovery from the public. To try to get it swept under the rug in the way Gran had. But she had the opportunity to make different decisions. To trust God to help her handle it and trust people like Dean to do their job. Gran had trusted no one, not even God, to help her through the difficult situations she'd faced.

"She shouldn't have said that," Lance said, his voice tight with anger. "That's not very fair."

"No, she's right. I should have told them about the letter right away. If I'd opened it as soon as I'd found it, this wouldn't have happened the way it did today. I kept a secret, just like Gran kept her secrets."

"You did what you thought was best."

"Yes, but it really wasn't what was best for everyone. Just what was best for me. I didn't want to have to deal with whatever Gran revealed about our mother. I am probably the only one who didn't want to know where she was or what had happened to her."

"Why is that?" Lance asked. "Why don't you want to know?"

Jessa sat silent for a minute staring out the front windshield. "I'm not sure exactly. I think because I had no interaction with her until she came to drop Violet, Laurel and Cami off. By that time, I was already almost six years old. Gran rarely, if ever, spoke of her and in my mind—and heart—Elizabeth was never my mother. I saw what the girls looked like when she brought them to the manor. Their hair was all tangled and dirty. Their clothes were ripped. Violet's were too small. Cami and Laurel's clothes were too big. And they were so thin. It took Violet a while to realize she didn't have to feed them. That she didn't need to make bottles for Cami. Elizabeth was a horrible mother to them. Why would I want anything to do with her? She just kept making bad choices after bad choices."

"I didn't realize," Lance said. "I can see how you might have thought having a woman like that in your lives wouldn't be a good thing."

"I just didn't want the others, especially Violet, to get hurt again. Violet has the most memories of her and for weeks after Elizabeth left them, I'd find her sitting on the front porch watching the driveway. I even heard her ask Gran once when Mama was coming back. When I saw the envelope from Gran all I could think was that Violet didn't need this right now. If Elizabeth had gotten her life back together, she would have come back to the manor. Since she never showed up, I assumed she was still living that wretched life she'd chosen."

"Will you go see her?"

"I don't know. Right now I need to focus on this," Jessa said as she lifted the letter. "And figure out what needs to be done. I'm sure Violet will go see her right away. I'll see how I feel a little later." She paused. "I have a hard time forgiving her for everything she's done to us."

"I understand that," Lance said. "But sometimes not forgiving does more harm to the person who won't forgive than it does to the other person."

Jessa knew he was right, but she didn't want to get into that right then. "I need to call Stan and see what he says."

When Lance didn't say anything further, Jessa found Stan's number in her contact list and placed the call. She explained to him what had happened and then listened as he gave her instructions with regards to what to do if the police wanted to ask questions of them. Not that any of them would have any answers. As best she could tell, most of this went down when they were in school, and Lily had been too young to know what was going on even though she would have been at the manor that day. The only one who might have known what was going on would have been Sylvia.

After promising to call him with an update or if they needed him, Jessa hung up and rested her head back against the seat. She closed her eyes and willed herself to relax. Music filled the cab of the truck and once again Jessa recognized the group from earlier.

She didn't know if Lance had chosen that song in particular or if it had just been the next one in the playlist, but the words sank deep into her soul.

When peace, like a river, attendeth my way, When sorrows like sea billows roll;

Whatever my lot, Thou hast taught me to say, It is well, it is well with my soul.

Peace had been elusive in the months since Gran's death. And things had truly not been well with her soul in quite some time. She had said all the right words when Violet had needed encouragement, and she'd offered sage advice to Laurel and Matt during their rough patch, but now that she was facing her own very real struggle, Jessa felt weak with no peace in her soul.

Though Satan should buffet, though trials should come, Let this blest assurance control,

That Christ hath regarded my helpless estate, and hath shed His own blood for my soul.

It is well with my soul, It is well, it is well with my soul.

The four part male harmony of the group drew out the words, and Jessa experienced the song in a way she never had singing it in church. It was what she wanted. To be able to say it was well with her soul. In spite of everything going on around her, that she had that peace God offered, and it was well with her soul.

She felt a hand cover hers where they were clenched together in her lap. Without opening her eyes, she unclasped them and allowed Lance to intertwine his fingers with hers. Strangely enough, though he was the one who had hurt her most deeply in the past, right then, he was the one she wanted by her side. She knew her family was angry with her for keeping the letter secret, so his support meant that much more.

They spent the next hour of the trip not talking; only music filled the silence. It wasn't until Lance's phone rang that he removed his hand from hers.

"Hey, Josh. What's happening there?" Lance asked.

Jessa opened her eyes and turned her head to watch him as he spoke on the phone. With his face in profile to her, she could study him without him being aware. She remembered riding with him in his car when they'd first been dating. It had been amazing to her back then how someone like Lance would have been interested in her. He was handsome, outgoing and popular. She had been reserved and gawky, but somehow he'd seen past all that, and soon they'd realized they had more in common than they had thought.

Lost in the past, Jessa didn't move fast enough when he ended the call and glanced over to find her watching him.

✺ Chapter Seventeen ✺

LANCE raised an eyebrow, but when he spoke, it was about the call. "Josh said Dean is out there now with his deputies. They've cordoned off the area, and a team should be there shortly to begin going through the dirt to collect the body and evidence. It sounds like Violet has already told him who the body is."

"What a mess," Jessa said. "And I don't care what that contract you had with Gran said, we're not building a gazebo there now. If there's some kind of penalty, I'll make it up to you out of my own money."

"We'll deal with that later," Lance told her. "Right now we've got an hour to go, and to be honest, I'm hungry. My burger is probably cold, but one of Kroll's burgers cold is better than a lot of hot ones."

Jessa opened the containers to find his burger and held it out to him. She wasn't starving, but knew that it was probably better to eat something now because once they got back to the manor, there would be lots of other things to do besides eat.

৵৽৶

Lance didn't bother to try to maintain a conversation with Jessa while he ate. He was still trying to figure everything out. She was as complex a woman as she had been a teenage girl. Back then it had been one of the things that had attracted him to her. He liked that she'd had more on her mind than what clothes were most stylish and who liked whom. He knew that being part of the Collingsworth family came with an expectation, but it seemed to have been put there more by their own grandmother than by the town.

Julia Collingsworth had expected a lot from them. Good grades. No getting into trouble. Helping out at businesses in the town. She had set the bar high for her girls. Out of all of them, he had seen that Jessa had tried the hardest to reach it. And he could see now that she still bore the weight of the family name and the expectations her grandmother had placed upon her from very young. The question was if she would turn out like Julia, keeping secrets and sacrificing her own happiness for others, or would she realize that honesty was the best policy, and that she could find joy in her spiritual life as well as her personal life without the world falling apart.

"I have some drinks in the cooler back there if you're thirsty," Lance said gesturing toward the back seat. "Hopefully they're still cold."

Jessa leaned over the seat. "What did you want?"

He told her his preference, and she turned back around with his drink and a bottle of water in her hands. She opened his drink before handing it to him.

"Thanks." He kept his eyes on the road as he drank his soda. They were nearing Collingsworth with only twenty miles left to go. He had no idea what awaited them. Given the confrontation Jessa had experienced with Violet, it was going to be even more complicated. But at least focus had turned off them for the time being.

He still wasn't sure how to respond to her challenge that

he do the job for the cost only. He could understand why she would want some type of reassurance that he wasn't just in it for the money, but his workers had families who depended on him being able to pay them a decent salary. Sometimes that meant he took a bit of a loss on one job, but would try to make it up on the jobs he could. The money from this job would have provided a nice cushion for the months ahead. Having just come through a difficult time in the economy, he had been looking forward to that extra to help him out, but now he didn't know what to do.

Lance glanced at Jessa. Her brow was furrowed, and tension had tightened her features. "Are you going to be okay?"

"Of course," she said without hesitation, but not a lot of conviction.

"And you and Violet?" he asked.

He heard her sigh. "I hope we'll be okay. All I can do is apologize. I thought I was doing the right thing at the time, but I know that sounds so much like what Gran has said in every letter she's written revealing her secrets. I need to learn from her mistakes."

"I think you need to understand you're not responsible for them anymore. None of them. They're all of age now. It was different for your grandmother because she *was* legally responsible for each of you. The best thing to do is let them make their own decisions about things. You can't protect them from life. They're living it now, and I think they're doing a pretty good job. Laurel seems happy with Matt. And Violet has gotten herself engaged to a good man. Trust them."

"You're right, of course, but it's easier said than done. I mean, you know about family responsibility. You were ready to get married because of your brother. I'm guessing you still take care of David even though he is your older brother."

Lance could hardly argue with her, but he was trying to get David to stand on his own two feet and take responsibility for his family. "I do know the feeling. I mean, I even feel responsible for my dad."

"It's hard to just step back from it," Jessa said. "Over the past few years I took on more and more of the responsibility for Rose and Lily. Gran's health wasn't great, and she seemed more than willing to let me take over. I didn't mind, but I never was their mother in any sense of the word, so I can't even claim that role and the rights that would come with it. Rose has Laurel, and Lily is of legal age now. No one needs me anymore."

She said it in a very matter of fact way, but Lance sensed the sadness and pain in that statement. "Well, that's where you're wrong. They all need you, just in a different role than you're used to playing. They need you as an older sister, not a guardian or a parent. It might take some adjusting, but I think you'll like that role even better than the one you've had."

He wanted to tell her that he needed her too, but knew it wasn't the right time for that statement. He hoped and prayed that there would be a right time for it in the near future.

As they approached the outskirts of Collingsworth, he turned onto the highway that bypassed the town to the north and took them to the manor. Lance slowed and pulled to the side of the road to stop just shy of the driveway.

"What's wrong?"

He turned to meet Jessa's questioning gaze. "I just want to give you a minute to prepare yourself."

"I've had a couple of hours to do that," Jessa pointed out.

"Okay. Then let me pray about this situation." He held out his hand and after a brief hesitation, Jessa took it. He lowered their clasped hands to the console between them and closed his eyes. The prayer was brief and to the point, asking God for guidance to deal with what lay ahead and that it would be resolved quickly without too many delays or legal issues.

After he finished, he gave her hand a squeeze and released it. "You're not alone in this. I'll be with you each step of the way. Okay?"

She nodded and took a noticeable deep breath. "Let's do this."

The first thing Jessa noticed as Lance drove the truck around the bend of the driveway was that there were a lot fewer cars than she had expected. In fact, it looked like it was just the family's vehicles and the squad cars from the sheriff's office.

"Where is everyone?" she asked.

"Josh said he thought he should send them home, and I agreed. I figured it would be easier for the sheriff's people to do their stuff if fewer people were around. And most likely the guys wouldn't have been interested in working with all this going on."

Lance parked the truck and got out. She had her door open by the time he got around to the passenger side. He waited as she climbed out and then shut the door. "I guess they're around the back."

Jessa headed toward the back corner of the house, aware of Lance close by her side. She wouldn't want to admit it to anyone, but his presence calmed her. Just knowing he was there with her helped keep the panic over what was to come at bay.

As they neared the back yard, they saw a group of people gathered near the tree line. Lance placed his hand on the small of her back as they moved in that direction. Violet spotted them, but she stayed where she was, arms crossed. Dean must have sensed a change in her demeanor though because he turned and began to walk in their direction with another man.

"I'm going to talk with Josh," Lance said as Dean approached. The two men shook hands as they passed.

"Jessa, this is Sheriff Billings. We've had to call in outside help given how closely I'm tied to the case. Sorry you had to end your trip this way."

"Not your fault. I could have prevented all this if I'd just read the letter sooner."

Dean rested his hands on his hips. "Speaking of the letter, may we have it?"

Jessa pulled it from her purse and handed it to him. "Have you contacted Sylvia?"

"Sylvia?" Dean asked. He glanced at the letter but then handed it to the man standing next to him.

"She would have to have known what happened that day. Even if Jonathan hadn't told her any details, she would have been here at the house watching Lily. I'm positive Gran wouldn't have taken the baby with her. And we older girls were in school."

The other sheriff looked up from the letter. "Do you remember anything from back around that time?"

Jessa gazed past Dean to the wooded area where the gazebo was to have been built. "I've been trying to remember. Of course, I recall our mother coming with her boyfriend and Lily, but her departure... I did think it was odd she left without saying goodbye, but then I thought maybe she said goodbye to the other girls but not to me, because they were her daughters more than I was."

"What do you mean?"

"I never spent any time with her. As soon as I was born, Gran took me, and Elizabeth left. Violet, Laurel and Cami had more time with her. Even Lily was with her for a few months." Jessa glanced to where Violet stood, her back to them now. "Violet might have a better recollection of what happened back then. She cared about her."

Dean shook his head. "She doesn't remember much. Just coming home one day, and Sylvia telling them that Elizabeth had left, and your grandmother had to go away for a few days as well."

"That's pretty much what I remember. Which is why Sylvia might have more answers." Jessa gestured to the letter. "That makes it pretty clear that Jonathan helped Gran with the body."

"Okay. We'll head over to see Sylvia," Dean said. "A couple of my men are here with the crime scene people to work through the dirt to see what else they can find. Let me know if anything else comes to mind."

Dean started to move past her, but Jessa laid her hand on his arm to stop him. "Could we be facing legal charges or anything for this?"

"You were all too young when this occurred. Sad to say, the only one who might is Sylvia. If she knew about it and said nothing, the district attorney may choose to prosecute."

Jessa shook her head. "I hope it doesn't come to that. She doesn't deserve to be the one left holding the ball. Do I need Stan to be there when you question her?"

The men exchanged glances then Dean said, "No harm in giving Stan a head's up. We'll have to work through this like any other case, although I won't have as active a role because of my connection to you guys. I'll make sure she's able to call him if I think it's necessary."

Jessa gave Dean Stan's contact info and then watched the two men walk toward the front of the house. When she turned her attention back to the group of people, she was suddenly at a loss as to what to do. Laurel stood with Violet and Cami, their backs to her. Will was with Matt, Josh and Dean looking at the mound of dirt and the now silent piece of machinery that had been brought in to dig the foundation.

It was just like when they'd been children. More often than not, Violet, Laurel and Cami had huddled together to play and often to sleep. Jessa had never been part of that tightknit group even though individually she'd had a connection of sorts with each one. But there were times, many times, when it was just the three of them together and her by herself. Over the past few months, she'd begun to feel like they were a family, but then she'd gone and ruined it all by keeping secrets, just like Gran.

Figuring she'd done all the damage she could, Jessa turned and walked past the back of the manor, past the trailers to the road leading to her greenhouse. She was angry at herself for allowing any of this to hurt. She shouldn't have been surprised that Gran had one last big secret. She shouldn't have been surprised that she messed stuff up with Violet and found herself on the outside looking in once again.

Without a care for her white pants or the blouse that had never seen the inside of the greenhouse before, Jessa pulled out several terracotta planters. When all else failed, she planted flowers. They weren't huge money makers, but once they had grown and had blossoms, people seemed happy to pay a few bucks for them.

Having planted these hundreds of times before, Jessa didn't need to pay too much attention to what she was doing, but her thoughts were roaming in directions that she didn't like, and yet she couldn't control them. There had only been one other time in her life when she'd felt like so much of a failure. When Lance had broken up with her and then got engaged so quickly, Jessa had felt like she'd failed to be a good enough girlfriend. Gran had assured her the problem was with Lance, not her. Of course now, Jessa knew the problem had been with Gran, but it didn't stop her from feeling the same way again.

She'd failed to protect her family. If she'd read the letter sooner, this could have been handled in a better way. Maybe her relationship with Violet and the others would still be intact. She tried to tell herself it didn't matter. She'd still go on with her life. They all would have left her and the manor eventually anyway. Lily might be the only one to stay around, but the others had their own lives, and she hadn't really been a part of them until recent months. They would go back to their lives, and she would have hers. Alone most likely, because Lance would realize, sooner or later, that he didn't want to spend the time and energy to get beyond the wall that was now firmly in place around her heart.

A tear dripped onto her hand. Jessa shook her head. "No tears," she murmured. "No tears."

When another one slid down her cheek, she brushed at it with her fingers, recalling too late that they were covered in dirt. She braced her hands on the work bench and bent her head. "Oh, Gran, why did you do this?"

Grief, anger, and fear flowed through her body and caused tears to fall more rapidly. She sobbed in a way she hadn't in many years. The heartbreak and betrayal she felt now, though coming from a different place than all those years ago, still ripped at her very being.

She was alone. So very alone.

Her legs suddenly gave way, and she sank to the dirt floor of the greenhouse, wrapping her arms around her knees. Losing control was something Jessa hated, and though she fought against it, she couldn't win this battle. All the emotion she'd been holding in for months flooded her, and there was no way for her to stop it now. It had to be felt. It had to be purged.

When arms closed around her, Jessa knew immediately who held her. The scent she'd enjoyed in the truck earlier wrapped around her as surely as his arms did. She didn't want him to see her this way. Weak. Shattered. A mess. But instead of fighting it, she allowed herself to sink into his embrace, to rest against the strength of his chest within the security of his arms.

Kneeling next to her, he tucked her head beneath his chin and held her tightly. Jessa had never been held that way before, even when they'd been together. But it was like he knew how close she was to falling completely apart and was doing his best to hold her together.

As the emotion began to dissolve, drifting away on soft intakes of breath, Jessa still stayed within Lance's embrace. Maybe she wasn't alone after all. Maybe, in spite of the things she'd said earlier in the day, he still wanted them to have a second chance. She lifted her head and met his gaze. The depth of emotion she saw there grabbed her heart.

Could she trust him again? Was this really what was best for them? To be together once more?

He had kissed her before, but when he lowered his head to press his lips to hers this time it was completely different. There was none of the giddy excitement she'd felt as a teenager. This time there was a heat that burned not just her body but her soul. And it felt right. Like she'd been waiting for this forever.

When he moved back from her, she waited for him to speak first. He brushed hair back from her face. "I know I keep asking this, but are you okay?"

This time Jessa shook her head. "I'm not, but I will be. It's just going to take some time. I made some mistakes, and I have to accept the consequences for that. I needed this, I think."

Lance stood, bringing her to her feet. He kept one arm around her waist as he looked down at her. "I'm sorry if I jumped the gun a little there. I don't want to pressure you. You have enough going on. Just know that I'm here for you."

His words warmed her heart and the loneliness she'd been feeling slowly faded. "Thank you."

"Are you ready to face the world?" Lance asked. "I think Laurel actually has supper made for us all."

Food didn't sound too appealing nor did spending time with her sisters, but Jessa wasn't one to run from confrontation. "Let's go."

As they walked along the road back to the trailer, Jessa looked down and saw the dirt all over her capris and realized what a mess she must be. "Guess I'd better clean up before dinner. I must be a sight."

Lance smiled. "A beautiful one."

Uncertain how to respond, Jessa glanced away. "Usually I wear my grubbies when I work in the greenhouse. I'm not afraid of dirt or mess, but this is a little more drastic."

As they came around the corner of Lance's trailer, they spotted the rest of the group gathered there already. Jessa fought the urge to smooth her hair and brush the dirt from her pants. "I'm going to clean up. I'll be back in a few minutes."

In the quiet of the trailer, Jessa grabbed a fresh set of clothes from the small chest of drawers. She decided to go ahead and take a quick shower to wash the mess away once she saw how dirty she really was.

"Jessa?"

Clean clothes in hand, Jessa turned from the drawers to see Violet in the doorway. Uncertain what she wanted, but not in the mood for further argument, Jessa said, "I think I'm going to take a quick shower. Too much dirt to get rid of with just a wash cloth. Go ahead and eat without me."

Violet held up a hand. "They're starting to eat already. I wanted to talk to you."

Jessa nodded but didn't say anything.

"I want to apologize for what happened earlier. I shouldn't have said what I did. I didn't mean to hurt you."

Jessa swallowed hard. She'd been so certain Violet would stay angry with her that the apology shocked her. "I'm sorry too. I should have given you the letter right away."

Violet's brown eyes filled with tears. "I love you, Jessa. I know that you've never really felt you were a sister to me like Cami and Laurel, but you are. You've always been my big sister, and I hate myself for how I acted earlier. I was wrong."

"You had every right to be angry with me, but I hope we can move past that. And I promise to be better about not making decisions on the important stuff by myself. Lance told me that even though no one needs me in the role of parent like Gran was, you still need me in the role of sister. Just like I need each of you. Was he right?"

Violet nodded. "Definitely. Even now, more than ever, we

need to stick together. We will disagree and even fight, but always know that, at the end of the day, you are my sister, and I love you."

"I love you too." Jessa took a step toward her and then paused. "I guess we can wait on the hug until I've showered."

"Sounds good. I'll make sure they keep food for you."

As Jessa stepped into the small shower and let the water wash away the dirt from her face, arms and legs, the last of the hurt washed away as well. When she stepped out of the trailer a little while later, Jessa felt stronger and more secure. And at peace. She knew that God had worked in her relationship with Violet and even with Lance. She would have made a mess of both if God hadn't been a part of it. Where it would go with Lance, she wasn't sure yet, but at least with Violet, she knew they would be forever sisters.

The next couple of days were spent dealing with more questions and watching as the investigators continued to unearth parts of the skeleton of Scott Lewis. Jessa could only imagine what the family was feeling now that they had been notified. She knew from Violet that they had been searching for him over the years, but this was no doubt not the result they'd been hoping for.

It was overwhelming to try to reign in her natural tendency to protect her family, much like Gran had done. But she was trying to let everything run its course without her interference. She would not stand in the way of what needed to happen in order for them to get past all of this.

By early Saturday afternoon, the forensics team let them know that they had finished. The skeleton had been relatively easy to recover since it had been buried immediately and not disturbed in all those years. The somewhat surprising discovery had been the envelope of cash found with him. Apparently Gran either hadn't instructed Jonathon to retrieve it or just hadn't cared about it.

Lance had shut down work on the manor for the rest of

the week as well, so there had been one less thing to deal with. It wasn't good for the timetable of the renovations, but Jessa had agreed it was necessary.

Now with the law enforcement presence gone and no workers on the grounds, a blanket of silence settled over the area with only the sounds of nature. Unfortunately, without anything else to think about right then, Jessa's thoughts turned to Lance. Since that time in the greenhouse, he had been true to his word and had been there as she'd dealt with everything that had cropped up as part of the investigation. But something had changed. Gone was the flirtatiousness he'd showed towards her at times. Gone were the smiles and winks. Even in the evenings when he could have spent time alone with her, he didn't seek her out, but instead had just stayed with the group as they'd socialized in the area outside the trailers.

Maybe it was just because of everything else going on, but Jessa couldn't help but wonder if he was rethinking his desire to see if there was still anything between them. The only way to know for sure would be to ask him. And while the thought of what his possible response might be caused a pit to form in her stomach, she needed to know. Figuring she'd find him in the manor, she climbed the back porch steps and walked into the kitchen. She stood for a moment, listening. There was no sound coming from anywhere in the building. She walked through to the staircase and called out a greeting to the second floor, but there was no response.

Finally, she headed out the front door and came to a stop on the front porch when she realized that his truck was gone. When she'd been on the phone with Stan earlier, she'd heard some vehicles start up and leave, but hadn't realized that one of them was Lance's. Hoping he'd just gone into town, Jessa made her way around to the trailers.

❧ Chapter Eighteen ❧

MATT and Laurel were sitting at one of the picnic tables talking. They both looked up at her approach. The seriousness of their expressions alarmed her at first, but then Laurel smiled and asked, "So, have you heard about Lance's proposal for Matt?"

Jessa sat down next to Laurel. "Dare I say yes? And that I was asked to keep it a secret until he talked to you?"

Laurel patted her hand. "This is an example of a good secret."

"What do you think about it?" Jessa asked, her gaze going to Matt.

Matt shrugged. "To be honest, I'd been praying for a way to get Laurel back closer to you guys. But I'd also been praying for something for me because I couldn't just sit around with nothing to do. Lance's offer is...amazing."

Jessa rested her arms on the picnic table. "How soon do you have to give him an answer?"

"He said to take as much time as we needed. Laurel has already let the school know she wouldn't be back to teaching for at least this year, so she's fine. I'm going to have to talk to my supervisor. I hate to leave him high and dry, but I think that in this current economy, there will be people available to fill my position." Matt grinned. "I know I'm not irreplaceable."

Laurel grabbed his hand. "You are to me."

"I'd better be," Matt replied as he lifted her hand to his lips.

"Okay, I'll leave you two to your love fest," Jessa said with a smile. "But first, do either of you know where Lance is?"

Laurel shook her head, but Matt said, "Oh yeah. He's en route to Fargo. He and Josh left a little while ago. He asked me to let you know because you were busy."

"Okay. Thanks." Still not sure how she felt about Lance not letting her know he was leaving, Jessa headed for the trailer. Was he planning to come back today? Or was he in Fargo for the rest of the weekend.

With nothing else demanding her attention right then, she might as well do her rounds of the garden and the shop. And try her best not to think about why Lance had left for Fargo without talking to her first.

As she was leaving the shop after talking with Missy, her phone alert for a text message went off. She tried not to feel disappointed when she saw it was from Maura and not Lance.

She paused on the sidewalk to check it out. *Dinner tonight? It's that time of year again. *smile**

Jessa stared down at the message then lifted her head, trying to recall the date. She laughed when it came to mind.

There had been so much going on she'd completely forgotten her own birthday. And apparently so had everyone else except Maura. Not that that was surprising. Gran hadn't been a big believer in celebrating birthdays. Jessa supposed she could understand since each birthday was a reminder of the bad decisions her daughter had made. Because of that, their birthdays had usually consisted of them being allowed to pick their favorite meal and a single gift from Gran.

To this day, Jessa was more apt to forget her birthday than remember it each year. The only year she was guaranteed to remember it was the year she was supposed to renew her driver's license. Sometimes Lily remembered, but usually it was just Maura who insisted on making something out of the occasion.

If you insist. lol Jessa texted back glad, in a way, that she wouldn't have to be sitting around all evening wondering about Lance.

I do. As I do every year.

Okay. Time and place?

Once Maura texted her the information, Jessa got into her car. As she arrived at the manor, another text came through from Maura. *Why don't you come get ready at my place? I've got a nice tub...*

The thought of a nice long bath appealed to Jessa, so she told her she'd be there shortly. She gathered up her things and let Laurel know she wouldn't be there for supper. They'd already agreed that everyone would be on their own for supper, but Jessa wanted to let her know regardless. Her sister was no doubt glad for the break.

"I'm going to leave to you to a little peace and quiet," Maura told her when she arrived. "I have to run a couple of errands, so you feel free to take as long as you need. My birthday present to you. A little pampering."

Jessa smiled. "Probably the best gift you could have gotten me this year."

"I've left some of the bath stuff you told me once you liked." Maura gave her a quick hug. "I'll be back in an hour or so."

Even with all the negative weighing on her, Jessa was determined to focus on the positive...for a while at least. She ran the bath with her favorite bubble bath, thankful that Maura had indulged in one of those deep tubs when she'd redone her bathroom the previous year. After setting her phone to her favorite playlist, Jessa sank into the warm water, leaned back and closed her eyes.

Thank you, God, for Maura.

She let her mind run through all the people in her life and expressed thanks for each one. For in spite of everything, with or without Lance, she was still more blessed than she realized most of the time. Gran, too, had been blessed, but it seemed she'd never taken the time to appreciate it. Jessa resolved that as she began this next year of her life, she wouldn't become like Gran. She would be a grateful person, who realized the blessings in her life and embraced them.

ॐ

"Well, that sucked." Lance didn't use the phrase often, but it more than applied in this situation.

"You can say that again," Josh agreed.

Lance pulled the truck out of the driveway of his house, wishing for all the world he hadn't decided to drop by when he and Josh had come into town. Since he hadn't made it to his office on Wednesday when he'd been in with Jessa, he'd decided to come today since Jessa had been busy making phone calls and there was nothing for him to do at the manor.

The first mistake he'd made had come when he'd decided to drop by the house. Daphne had thought they were home for the weekend. His second mistake had been telling her that they were just there to pick up a couple of things. And the final mistake he'd made, which had resulted in an estrogen explosion of tears and sobbing, had been asking how the house hunting was going.

"Do you ever wonder about Dave's safety around that woman?" Josh asked.

Lance sighed. "Lately, yes. And I wonder how those kids are going to turn out with a mom like that."

"She's nuts," Josh said. "And I mean that in the kindest way, since I know a little bit about stuff like that."

Lance glanced over at his cousin. "Was Emma that bad?"

Josh frowned. "Worse. I'm still not sure what happened, just that after the miscarriage, she lost her mind."

Lance didn't ask any more questions. He knew most of the details of what had happened around the time of Emma's death and didn't want to drag it all out again. "I really think that once they get settled in their own home, and Dave shows her that he can care for their family, she'll settle down. At least that's what I'm hoping."

"If not, Dave needs to look into getting her some help before she gets much worse."

Lance nodded. Relief filled him as they passed the outskirts of town and left Fargo in his rear view mirror. It would be good to get back to Collingsworth, even if it meant sleeping on the bed in the trailer instead of his expensive, comfortable bed at the house.

"What's been up with you and Jessa these past couple of days?" Josh asked.

"What?" Lance looked away from the road for a second.

"I know there's been lots going on, but it seems like you've changed your mind about her."

Lance shook his head. "I haven't. Why would you think that?"

"Mainly because you've changed you interact with her."

Lance mulled over his cousin's words. It was true things had turned serious over the past few days. He had thought it would be a little inappropriate to continue flirting with her in the light of all that had gone, but he'd done his best to keep his promise to be there for her. He hadn't wanted her to think he was pressuring her after that kissed they'd shared in the greenhouse. He knew it was important that she deal with everything else first. He'd be waiting when it finally settled down.

But if Josh thought he'd changed his mind, did Jessa think the same thing? Lance gave his head an exasperated shake. Had he messed up with her yet again? There was nothing he could do about it now. Figuring it out over the phone with Josh listening in wasn't exactly ideal, but he'd make sure he talked with her later.

The CD changer in the truck moved onto the next one in the queue before Lance realized it was Josh's. He'd forgotten to take it out after his trip with Jessa. He tried not to play it when Josh was around in case it brought back bad memories, but as he reached out to press the button to skip it, his cousin stopped him.

Lance looked at him as Josh said, "It's okay. I think I'd like to listen to it."

And as the miles passed beneath the truck, for the first time in forever, Lance heard Josh use the voice God had blessed him with. A smile curved his lips as his cousin sang along with himself and the others in the group. His talent could have taken him to the heights of gospel music, Lance was sure, and maybe there was still a chance Josh could once again rise from the ashes of his life. And as much as he wanted to keep Josh close, he also wanted him to be able to bless people with the talent God had given him.

When they reached the manor a couple of hours later, the first thing that struck Lance as they pulled to a stop was the absence of vehicles. The only ones there were Laurel's car and Josh's truck. As they walked toward the trailers, there was no activity outside them. Lance knocked first on Matt's trailer and then Jessa's with the same result at both. No answer.

He pulled out his phone and texted Matt, not wanting to horn in on a family thing, if that's why they were all gone, but still a bit worried. Given all that had transpired over the past week, he couldn't dismiss anything.

Just got back to deserted manor. Everything okay?

It didn't take long for an answer to show up on his screen. *Yep. Celebrating Jessa's birthday. Come join us.*

ᴄ Chapter Nineteen ᴐ

*J*ESSA'S *birthday*? Lance felt like he was going to be sick. How had he not known it was her birthday? No one had said anything about it either. Of course, when they'd been together, they'd celebrated his birthday in October, Christmas and Valentine's Day, but by the time the school year was done, so were they. They'd never celebrated her birthday, and he wasn't even sure she'd ever told him when it was.

"What's wrong?" Josh asked.

"Nothing, I guess. They're out celebrating Jessa's birthday."

Josh's eyes widened. "Did you know it was her birthday?"

"Nope," Lance said with a shake of his head. "They're inviting us to join them."

"I'm up for it if you are," Josh told him.

"But I can hardly show up empty-handed," Lance said with a frown. "Especially if she thinks what you think because of how I've been acting the past few days. Why didn't anyone tell me about this sooner?"

Josh laid a hand on his arm. "Just let it go, cuz. Let's go and have a good time. If you want, we can stop and get her some flowers and a card."

Lance nodded and texted back to Matt to ask where they were and how much longer they were going to be there.

"Looks like we won't be too late," Lance said when Matt replied. "But if we're going to stop for a gift, we'd better get going."

When they walked into the restaurant a half hour later, Lance was feeling a bit frustrated. First to have been caught off guard and then trying to find the perfect gift for the woman he loved, but had no idea if he had a relationship with. He'd ended up with just a card and the hope he could get her something better the next day.

Josh elbowed him as the hostess led them to a private room at the back of the restaurant. "Stop scowling."

"What?"

"You're scowling. Makes it look like you're not happy to be here."

Lance blew out a breath and then smiled. "Better?"

Josh let out a snort, which confirmed he'd failed miserably at his attempt. But seeing his cousin laugh actually brought a genuine smile to his lips.

"There you go," Josh said.

Jessa looked around the room, surprised that Maura had been able to pull this off on such short notice. Being together with these people warmed her heart. After the week they'd all had, it was a blessing to be together like this and just relax. Of course, Josh and Lance weren't there, but from what Maura had said, she'd pulled it together quickly and they had already left. Something told Jessa Maura was just as glad and hadn't made any effort to get hold of Lance.

Trying not to focus on who wasn't there, Jessa turned her

attention to Gareth, who sat on her right. His presence had been a surprise since she hadn't given Maura more than his name. She suspected that Maura's intent was to encourage their intellectual connection to become something more. Jessa hadn't told Maura yet that there was never going to be anything between her and Gareth beyond friendship.

"Hey! Glad you guys made it." Jessa looked over at Matt's greeting in time to see the hostess lead Josh and Lance into the room.

Jessa's heart skipped a beat when her gaze landed on Lance. He was smiling that smile she loved so much as he clapped Matt on the shoulder. "Sorry we're late. Things in Fargo ran a bit longer than we had planned."

There were a couple of extra seats at the table, but from the look on Maura's face, she hadn't planned on these two being the ones to fill them.

"Looks like lover boy made it after all," Gareth said under his breath. "Lucky bloke."

Jessa smiled at him. "There's nothing there yet, and might not be. Only time will tell."

"Well, every minute that guy lets go by without laying claim to you is a loss. His loss."

"You're not really all that surprised there's nothing between you and me, are you?" Jessa asked him.

Gareth paused then gave her wink. "Nah. I enjoyed spending time with you, but as soon as I saw him, I knew it was going to be friends only. And I'm fine with that. Particularly after meeting Maura. She seems interesting."

Jessa couldn't help but laugh as she realized that they, in fact, would be a pretty good match. From their conversations, she knew that Gareth enjoyed traveling as much as Maura did. "Did you know she's been to Australia?" Jessa poked Maura, drawing her attention from Lance and Josh. "Hey. I was just telling Gareth about how you'd been to Australia. He's from there."

Maura shot one more look down the end of the table before turning her attention to Gareth. "I loved my time there."

"Why don't we switch seats," Jessa suggested to Maura. "Then you two can talk."

Maura didn't hesitate, and soon she and Gareth were conversing about their travels. And Jessa was out of view of Lance. Moving to Maura's seat placed her on the same side of the table as Lance so she didn't have to keep looking at him and wondering what was up. Hopefully she'd enjoy the meal a bit more that way.

Since moving over, Jessa was seated next to Laurel. Her younger sister gave her a curious look when she glanced over and saw they'd changed seats.

Jessa leaned close to her and whispered, "I think Maura and Gareth are hitting it off."

Laurel's gaze went to where Gareth and Maura sat, heads close together, talking intently. Thankfully she seemed to accept that as Jessa's reason for switching seats. When the waitress came back with their meals, she was temporarily confused by the addition of two more guests and the switching of seats. It didn't take her long to get it straightened out though.

Violet said grace for the meal, thanking God for Jessa and for the end of a stressful week, to which everyone said a hearty amen. As she was eating, Laurel handed her a couple of envelopes.

"What are these?"

"I don't know. Matt just handed them to me."

Jessa turned them over and recognized the handwriting on one. *Lance.* There was no way she was going to open it here. Who knew what was inside given his interactions with her over the past few days. She slipped them into her purse and resumed eating. For now, she was just going to enjoy having her whole family together for the first time ever, since

Will had never been a part of their gatherings in the past.

After they were finished eating, the staff brought out the cake Maura had ordered, and they sang for her. It had been the first time that Jessa had had a cake with so many candles, but happily posed for pictures before managing to blow out every single flickering flame.

"Jessa!" Rose exclaimed. "You have no boyfriends!"

Every head in the room turned toward the little girl.

"Um...what?" Jessa asked her, acutely aware of the silence in the room.

"Your candles. At school they say you know how many boyfriends or girlfriends you have by the number of candles left with flames," she explained. "You have none left."

"Now, that can't be right," Gareth said. "See, I'm one."

If anything, the silence grew heavier as Rose looked at him. "You're Jessa's boyfriend?"

Jessa stared first at Rose then at Gareth. What on earth was he thinking?

"Well, sure. I'm a boy, and I'm her friend. Doesn't that count?"

"I'm not sure. Have you kissed her?" Rose asked.

Gareth looked at her then, humor sparking in his eyes. Jessa gave what she hoped was an imperceptible shake of her head. Technically, he had kissed her...on the cheek. He winked at her then grinned as he turned his attention back to Rose.

"Not in the way you likely mean. So I guess that disqualifies me, but it might qualify someone else in the room."

Before anyone could pursue that, Jessa stood and grabbed the knife the waitress had brought in with the cake. "Do you want the flower, Rose?"

Sure that her cheeks were still burning, Jessa kept her

head down as Rose helped her remove the candles. Carefully she cut pieces and put them on the plates to be handed out. There was a flash of irritation as she worked, not necessarily at Gareth, although that was part of it, but at herself. She was acting like a teenager, blushing at the insinuations made by Gareth. The *does he like me or doesn't he* thoughts she'd had over the past couple of days didn't help. She should have been able to handle this with more maturity.

They were among the last to leave the restaurant by the time they finished with the cake. Jessa rode with Maura back to her house since she'd left her car there. She went in for a bit to thank her friend for the evening.

"Did you enjoy talking with Gareth?" she asked after gathering up her clothes and bath stuff from earlier.

"I did," Maura said with an emphatic nod. "He really did get you going there for a bit, didn't he?"

"Yeah. Quite the sense of humor he's got."

"You should have seen Lance's face," Maura commented. "I had a pretty good view of it."

"At that moment I didn't want to see *anyone's* face, to be honest."

"It *was* kind of funny, you have to admit."

Jessa lifted an eyebrow. "I do?"

"Ah c'mon. If anything, it shook Lance up a bit, and I'm thinking that's a good thing."

Jessa shrugged. "Who knows what's in Lance's mind right now. It's been a rough week for all of us."

"Well, just tell me that you're truly not interested in Gareth. I find I'm a bit fascinated by him in a way I haven't been in a very long time. But he was yours first, so just say the word, and I'll back off."

Jessa shook her head. "Nope. We talked and decided friendship was the best thing for us. He's all yours."

"Good. Nicest birthday present I've ever gotten when it

wasn't even my birthday."

She couldn't help but laugh at Maura then. "Thank you for the lovely evening."

Once back at the manor, Jessa carried her things to the trailer. Lights were still on, but as she stepped inside she could see they were getting ready for bed.

"Well, if it isn't the birthday girl," Cami remarked. "Nobody told me it was going to be a roast or I would have prepared something."

"Very funny," Jessa said. "That was more than enough."

"You mean you wouldn't have wanted me to talk about the time I caught you and Lance making out on the swing down by the lake?"

Jessa groaned. "Cami! We were not making out. Kissing maybe, but not making out."

"I'm having a hard time picturing that," Lily commented. "You and Lance?"

"I never heard about that," Violet said as she plopped down on the couch next to Cami and Lily. "Why didn't you tell me?"

Cami rolled her eyes. "Well, it just so happened that Jessa had enough on me to make my life very miserable if I told anyone."

"And I wasn't above using it either," Jessa added.

Violet elbowed Cami. "You still could have told me. I wouldn't have tattled to Gran." A grin spread across her face. "I'm just having fun imagining it all happening. The surprise when Cami found you guys. The threats. I'm sure it was hilarious."

It had happened pretty much as Violet had described, and Jessa started to laugh at the memory. Pretty soon the four of them were laughing. As they all sat there together, Jessa felt like it was a nearly perfect end to her birthday. Only Laurel was missing, but knowing that she was with the man she loved, made the absence acceptable.

In bed a short time later, Jessa opened Josh's envelope, smiling at the card covered in flowers with a simple birthday greeting within. She stared at Lance's. She wasn't sure she wanted to open it just yet. If it were similar in content to Josh's, she'd be disappointed and ending her birthday that way was not what she wanted. She would leave it for the next day.

The next morning they all showed up at their church in Collingsworth. Violet had gone early with Dean since he was ushering that day. She and Addy sat in a pew with Sylvia and Will. Matt led Rose and Laurel into the pew behind them. Cami followed Laurel, and Jessa brought up the rear. She'd only been seated a couple of minutes when movement at her end of the pew drew her attention. Lance stood there with Josh.

Jessa gave them a smile that she hoped didn't look too forced because her insides were quivering at the sight of Lance. She moved a little closer to Cami to make room for the two of them. He wore a perfectly pressed white dress shirt tucked into a pair of black slacks. And as he sat down next to her, she realized he smelled as good as he looked.

She felt a poke in her side, and when she turned, Cami nodded in Laurel's direction. Jessa leaned forward to talk with her. She felt her Bible begin to slip from her lap. Without looking, she grabbed it, so it didn't end up on the floor. Before she could say anything more to Laurel, the worship band began to play.

She moved back in the pew, her gaze going to Lance. He sat with his head bent. She looked down, and her heart skipped a beat when she saw what he held in his hands. When her Bible had slipped, the torn picture she'd put there over a week ago must have fallen out.

❧ Chapter Twenty ❧

JESSA knew he'd never seen the picture. For some reason, she'd never showed it to him, but he was staring at it now, holding the torn edges together. And then he turned the pieces over to reveal the back. Jessa gasped. In black marker, the words NEVER AGAIN were scrawled. One word on each side. She had completely forgotten what she'd written that night he'd broken up with her. And when she'd found it again, she hadn't turned them over. Looking at the picture itself had been painful enough.

Lance's thumb brushed across the words. Jessa reached out to take the pieces of the picture from him, but he moved them out of her reach and slid them into the breast pocket of his shirt. Jessa glanced to the front and saw that the team was moving in place to sing. There was nothing she could do now but wait.

"Everyone, please stand," the worship leader instructed as he took his place behind the microphone, guitar in hand.

Feeling sick to her stomach, Jessa stood. Hopefully, he would understand that it had been a heartbroken teenage girl who had ripped that picture and written those words. Of course, he might not understand why she still had them and why they were in her Bible, of all places.

She pressed a hand to her stomach and swallowed, trying to get past the dryness of her mouth to be able to sing. The worship team moved through the songs with ease. She noticed that while Lance sang along with the congregation, Cami did not. Jessa realized that Cami would most likely not know many of the songs if she wasn't attending church.

They sat down after the first group of songs, and Jessa tried to keep her focus on the person who read the announcements and the scripture. She put her offering in the basket when it was passed, aware with every movement of Lance beside her. After the second group of songs, the pastor got up to preach.

Jessa looked down at the bulletin, only then seeing the title of his sermon for the day. Joy in the Storm. *Really?* It was like the guy had gotten a glimpse of life that week and decided to preach right to her. Part of her wanted to ignore what he was saying, hating the idea of being preached at. But then she remembered how she'd felt in the truck coming back from Fargo. She had wanted to have peace and joy in the midst of everything that was going on. Maybe it wasn't the pastor who knew what she needed to hear, but God.

Bowing her head, Jessa tried to block out everything else but the words of the sermon.

"So often people will say, 'I'll be happy when this happens or that happens.' Maybe it's when they land their dream job. Buy their dream home. Marry their soul mate. Lose weight. Whatever it is that they've deemed essential to their happiness. How many years do these people lose waiting for their happiness to arrive?

"They need to trade in their pursuit of happiness for joy. In Psalm 32 it says, 'In Your presence is fullness of joy; At Your right hand are pleasures forevermore.' It's right there. In God's presence is fullness of joy. Don't we all want to be filled with joy? Spend time in God's presence. And at His right hand are pleasures forevermore. At His right hand...in

His presence...are pleasures forevermore.

"Don't wait for happiness to come your way, reach out and grab the joy that's right there waiting for you. When you realize that joy doesn't come from things, but from God, you are able to weather the storms that come. If you haven't experienced that joy from God, when the bad things come, you'll just see them as a step backward from whatever is that you've decided is your ultimate goal for happiness. Your car breaks down? Well, now it's going to take even longer to get your dream house. You get a bad grade at school? Will you ever be able to get your dream job? Your girlfriend breaks up with you? Will you ever find your soul mate? These things will fill you with despair if you haven't figured out how to fill your heart with joy and contentment in whatever situation you are in.

"The Bible actually tells us to be thankful for those trials. In James it says, 'My brethren, count it all joy when you fall into various trials.' Yes, that's right. Count it all *joy*. That's what God is telling us to do, but how many of us really can say that we are joyful in the midst of trials. I know I can't say that I do it every time. I try and sometimes fail, but when I find myself sliding into despair, I know what I've done wrong and have the choice to correct it."

Jessa heard the words and knew that too often she was waiting for that happiness to come her way. Or worse yet, she'd decided that in a lot of areas, it wasn't meant to be and had let despair creep into that part of her heart. She had no joy or peace when it came to how she had been raised without a loving family like Will. She felt it stood between her and happiness. She'd held herself apart from people, fearing the hurt because of what she'd experienced before. There was no joy there. And certainly no peace.

"So do you want that joy? Do you want peace for the storms of life? It's all right here." Jessa looked up in time to see the pastor lift his Bible into the air. "You must spend time with God, let Him fill your heart. Spend time in prayer. Spend time reading His word. Spend time listening."

The pastor didn't give an alter call or lead in prayer for raised hands, but as the worship team stood and began to play, the familiar tune grabbed at her heart, just as it had in the truck. She joined the congregation as they stood, and as the song progressed, she heard a voice, a beautiful male voice, rise above those around her. Jessa looked over, past Lance, and saw Josh, eyes closed with his hands raised singing the song, just as he had on the CD. She turned back and closed her eyes as well. Her voice wasn't nearly as good as Josh's, but the words came from her heart as they surely came from his.

> *My sin—oh, the bliss of this glorious thought!*
> *My sin, not in part but the whole,*
> *Is nailed to the cross, and I bear it no more,*
> *Praise the Lord, praise the Lord, O my soul!*
> *It is well with my soul, it is well,*
> *It is well with my soul.*

After the song had ended, the pastor stood to give the benediction. As he said the prayer, Jessa knew that she was going to trust God to fill her with peace, regardless of what was to come. She opened her heart fully to him, giving Him all the space He needed to work in her.

Before Jessa could say anything to Lance after the service, he and Josh got up and left. She turned to watch them walk up the side aisle the doors leading to the foyer. Not sure how to interpret his rapid exit, Jessa resolved that before the day was over, she would have some sort of resolution where Lance was concerned.

Lance didn't say anything as he started up the truck and pulled out of the church's parking lot. Thankfully Josh didn't seem to be in a chatty mood either. What he'd heard in the sermon that morning was nothing new to him. He knew he'd been struggling more with it lately, and it was in direct correlation to him not spending as much time with God. He'd allowed the busyness of his life to sidetrack his spiritual walk. His daily devotions have become his *"whenever I have*

a few minutes" devotions. Why should God bless him when he didn't give Him any position of importance in his life?

"Haven't heard you sing like that in church before," Lance said with a glance at Josh.

"Yeah. After hearing that CD yesterday and then the sermon... Singing it just felt right."

"I'm glad. It was a blessing for me to hear you sing like that. I've missed it."

"Me too."

When they pulled up at the manor, Lance didn't turn off the engine right away.

"Something wrong?" Josh asked.

"Would you pray with me? I need to talk with Jessa," Lance told him. He pulled out the torn picture and handed it to Josh. "That fell out of Jessa's Bible this morning. I hope the sermon wasn't preparing me for the worst, but I need prayer for the right words and attitude when I talk to her."

Josh readily agreed. Lance bent his head and listened with a grateful heart as his cousin prayed on his behalf asking God for wisdom and understanding. They had just ended their prayer when another car pulled up. Lance saw it was Jessa's and took a deep breath. The passenger door opened, and Cami got out and made her way toward the trailer. The driver's side opened more slowly, and when Jessa got out, she didn't follow Cami. Instead, she rounded the front of his truck and came to the door. Anticipating her arrival, Lance rolled down his window.

She pushed her sunglasses to the top of her head as she came close. "Can we talk?"

Lance glanced at Josh then back at Jessa. "Yes."

He turned off the truck and as he opened the door, she stepped back to give him room.

"Let's go to the lake," Jessa said. "There's more privacy there."

Lance nodded, remembering the spot she was talking about. In silence, they crossed the back yard, and he followed behind her along the dirt path that led to the lake. She didn't pause to enjoy the view, but went right to the swing and sat down on one end of it. Lance sat down on the other.

He held out the torn photograph. She stared at it for a moment before taking the pieces. He watched as she laid them on her lap, fitting the torn edges together.

"I didn't mean for you to see this," she said when she looked up at him. "I put it in my Bible last week. I thought I needed a reminder of how much you'd hurt me, so I could make sure it didn't happen again."

"Is that when you wrote on the back?" Lance asked.

She shook her head. "I did that when I ripped the picture. The night you broke up with me."

"I wish I could go back and do things differently. Or maybe I wouldn't be able to. Definitely I wouldn't get engaged again. That should never have happened, but I was just trying to fix everything for everyone. And in the process, even though it was never my intent, I made things even worse for you."

"I thought everything we'd had was a lie." Jessa looked down at the picture again. "That you'd been with her even while you were telling me you love me."

"I know how it looked but trust me, I meant it when I said I loved you." He rubbed the area just below his left collarbone. "My heart was broken then too. But I decided I wanted to always have a piece of you with me."

Jessa looked at him, her brows drawn together over her beautiful blue-green eyes. "What do you mean?"

"I took some of the money your grandmother paid me and did something for me." Lance undid a couple of the buttons of his shirt and moved the fabric aside so Jessa could see.

She stared for a long moment before reaching out to

touch the tattoo. "That's my design. Over your heart."

Lance covered her hand with his, capturing it against his chest. He wondered if she could feel the pounding of his heart. "Yes. Over my heart."

She looked up at him, her eyes damp. "What if there had been someone else?"

"I told myself that the minute I found someone who stirred my heart as much as you did, I'd get it removed. It never happened." Lance paused. "And now I don't want to ever remove it."

"So you really do want to see if there's still something between us," Jessa asked.

Lance lowered their hands from his chest, but didn't release his grasp on hers. "I already know, Jessa. But if you need time, I will give you that."

"We live so far apart now," Jessa said. "How can it work?"

"I know this is your home. I wouldn't ask you to give that up. My job isn't tied to Fargo. I do jobs all over the place. Sometimes I don't have to be on site as much as others." He smiled then. "Like this job. I really don't need to be here. Josh has it well in hand. I'm here for you. But if a job did require me to be away for a while, always know that I will be coming home to you as often and as soon as I can."

Jessa glanced in the direction of the manor. "Do you think maybe we can finally fill this house with love? I think it's been without it for so long."

"It's an empty shell right now," Lance said. "I think filling it with love is a wonderful idea."

Lance tugged her hand to bring her closer. "Do you think I can kiss you without fear of Cami interrupting?"

Jessa smiled, a twinkle in her eyes. "I hope so."

Lance began to lower his head, but then stopped. He pulled back slightly. "I don't want to rush you, Jessa. I know how I feel, but I need you to be sure too."

She slipped her hand along the back of his neck. "I'm sure too. I love you, Lance."

"I love you too, Jessamine." He pressed his lips to hers as her hand tightened on the back of his neck. It had been too long and yet Lance knew he would have waited forever for this.

When the kiss ended, he ran his fingertips along her jawline. "About the card I gave you last night..."

Jessa gave him a rather sheepish smile. "I actually haven't read it yet."

"Good," Lance said. "I need to add something to it. Or better yet, just toss it, and I'll get you a whole new one."

Jessa laughed. "This is all the birthday gift I need. I had asked God for joy and peace regardless of what happened between us."

"So did I," Lance told her. "I'm glad that the joy and peace can be there right along with our love."

"And I believe God will help us make that house a home with our love for each other and for Him."

"Without a doubt," Lance agreed as he lowered his head to seal that love with another kiss.

❧ *The End* ☙

OTHER TITLES AVAILABLE BY

Kimberly Rae Jordan
(Christian Romances)

Marrying Kate

Faith, Hope & Love

Waiting for Rachel (*Those Karlsson Boys: 1*)
Worth the Wait (*Those Karlsson Boys: 2*)
The Waiting Heart (*Those Karlsson Boys: 3*)

Home Is Where the Heart Is (*Home to Collingsworth: 1*)
Home Away From Home (*Home to Collingsworth: 2*)
Love Makes a House a Home (*Home to Collingsworth: 3*)
The Long Road Home (*Home to Collingsworth: 4*)
Her Heart, His Home (*Home to Collingsworth: 5*)
Coming Home (*Home to Collingsworth: 6*)

A Little Bit of Love:
A Collection of Christian Romance Short Stories

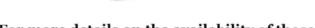

For more details on the availability of these titles,
please go to

www.KimberlyRaeJordan.com

Contact

Please visit Kimberly Rae Jordan on the web!
Website: www.kimberlyraejordan.com
Facebook: www.facebook.com/AuthorKimberlyRaeJordan
Twitter: twitter.com/Kimberly Jordan

Printed in Great Britain
by Amazon

51073487R00118